John Creasey's [...]
hundred million [...]
translated into [...]

Born in 1908, John Creasey had a home in Arizona, U.S.A., since more of his books were sold in the United States than in any other country. He also had his home in Wiltshire, England, and he virtually commuted between the two.

He travelled extensively, and was very interested in politics. He was founder of The All Party Alliance and fought four elections for this movement, advocating government by the best men from all parties and independents. Married three times, he had three sons. John Creasey died in June 1973.

**Also in the same series,
and available in Coronet Books:**

The Baron Series

The Baron in France
Salute for the Baron
Danger for the Baron
Nest Egg for the Baron
The Baron & the Missing Old Masters
The Baron Goes East
The Baron & the Unfinished Portrait
Frame the Baron
Last Laugh for the Baron
A Sword for the Baron
The Baron Goes Fast
Sport for the Baron

Black for the Baron

John Creasey
writing as ANTHONY MORTON

CORONET BOOKS
Hodder Paperbacks Ltd., London

Copyright © 1959 by the Executors
of John Creasey deceased
First Published by
Hodder and Stoughton Ltd 1959
Coronet Edition 1962
Second impression 1974

The characters in this book are entirely imaginary and
bear no relation to any living person.

This book is sold subject to the condition that it shall
not, by way of trade or otherwise, be lent, re-sold,
hired out or otherwise circulated without the publisher's
prior consent in any form of binding or cover other
than that in which this is published and without a similar
condition including this condition being imposed on the
subsequent purchaser.

Printed in Great Britain
for Coronet Books, Hodder Paperbacks Ltd.,
St Paul's House, Warwick Lane, London, EC4P 4AH
by Richard Clay (The Chaucer Press), Ltd.,
Bungay, Suffolk.

ISBN 0 340 18306 3

CONTENTS

Chapter		Page
1	MISSING MONEY	7
2	UNTRUTHFUL DAUGHTER	16
3	PROUD PARENT	25
4	UGLY FACTS	32
5	GUY	38
6	PROMISE	46
7	THE EVIDENCE	54
8	DANGER LIST	61
9	MANNERING	69
10	HIDING PLACE	76
11	CAR RIDE	85
12	TRUTH?	93
13	SECOND HIDING PLACE	100
14	MANNERING BLUFFS	109
15	PAST	116
16	PICTURE OF A MAN	124
17	DISTRESS	133
18	LORNA MANNERING	140
19	OLIVE BRANCH	148
20	MANNERING WAKES	156
21	BLANK WALL	164
22	THE BARON AGAINST TIME	171
23	CONCUSSION	179
24	COOL REASON	185

CHAPTER ONE

MISSING MONEY

ALICIA VANE went to the cash box uneasily, and hesitated before she touched it. Looking out of the window of the small office, she saw her husband loading early lettuce into a van, and Guy, their nineteen-year-old son, pushing a truck loaded with greenhouse tomatoes. The men were much alike in looks although Michael, her husband, was grey-haired at forty-four, and Guy's jet black hair was glistening in the morning sun. Each had exceptional single-mindedness, and they were intent only on one thing: getting the van loaded and into Gilston for the market, where they were sure to sell all the stock.

The red brick of the walled garden and the white of the newly painted greenhouses contrasted vividly. In front of Alicia's eyes were the twenty acres of fertile land on which they laboured—slaved would sometimes be a better word—so that soon they could buy more land and work it. Just in sight was Red House Farm, likely to be on the market in a year or so: buying that was the real objective of both father and son.

Alicia had never known them happier, for everything had gone right with the greenhouse produce this spring.

She herself had never been more uneasy.

She wasn't unhappy yet, but the seeds of unhappiness for them all lay in that black metal box, standing so openly on the desk. Of course some of the blame, if there were blame to apportion, was Michael's. He had always been too careless with money, left the box unlocked, seldom kept an accurate account, just left it to her to make up the figures at the end of the day.

She knew exactly how much money there should be in the box, but Michael didn't; and Alicia doubted whether Guy had more than a rough idea.

There should be thirty-nine pounds eleven shillings and five pence. Most of the notes would be crumpled and soiled from much handling.

She opened the box.

There was the money, quite neatly stacked, the silver in a blue bank envelope, the coppers loose, the notes apparently untouched. Yet she felt sure that the box was in a different position from the one where she had left it; and she had placed it deliberately, so that she could tell at a glance whether it had been disturbed.

She took out the money.

As she did so, she looked at the photograph of the whole family, taken last year during one of the weekends at Clay, the Dorset village where they liked to go because it was comparatively quiet. At one time they had spent three weeks every summer there, but recently only the odd week-end; there had been so much to do here.

Michael was standing in that curiously aggressive way of his, pipe jutting from his mouth, one hand on his hip, the other on Guy's shoulder. Guy was smiling, and had his arm round Hester's waist. Hester was looking unbelievably lovely, wearing what Guy called her beauty queen bikini. It was hard to believe that this young, vital, attractive creature was her daughter; just two years older than Guy.

In the photograph, she had her fair hair coiled up inside a bathing cap; in another, of Hester by herself, her hair was rippling down to her shoulders. That was Michael's favourite picture of his only daughter. It would not be just to say that he was consciously more fond of Hester than of Guy, but undoubtedly she meant more to him; she was their first child, whom they had very nearly lost in infancy.

The seaside photograph was a happy one, and the studio picture made Hester look as if she were full of zest, too.

She was.

She had been here twenty minutes ago, just before rushing off on her motor-scooter for Gilston and her day's work.

Alicia moved the box, abruptly, and let the lid fall back. She took out the pound notes and began to count them, but before she was half-way through she slowed down. Too obviously, some were missing. She began to count to herself:

". . . twenty-two, twenty-three, twenty-four. . . ."

Her voice trailed off.

There were thirty-four pounds here, including the ten-shilling notes, five less than when she had counted them only this morning. No one else had been here, only Michael, Guy and Hester could have touched the box—and she felt quite sure that only Hester had. During the past month, over twenty pounds had been taken. Michael, leaving the accounts to her, didn't know. Because it had been such a good spring, the money cashed was considerably up on last year, and unless she told him he would probably never know what was missing. She ought to, of course, but it would be a severe blow, and Alicia wasn't sure how he would react to it.

It might spark off a fit of rage.

It might spoil his absolute trust in his family, and that was the greater danger.

Of course he ought to be told.

"Why is she doing it?" Alicia found herself asking in a low-pitched, bitter voice. "She earns nearly ten pounds a week and gives me only three, so she should have plenty of money. If only I knew why."

The silence gave no answer.

The men were loading the last of the tomatoes. Suddenly Michael turned and came striding towards her, as always in a hurry, clenching his pipe, giving her a kind of half-fierce smile.

"Just off, sweet."

"Have you as much as you hoped?" Alicia asked.

"Twenty-eight pounds of tomatoes extra, and a couple of dozen lettuce. Nothing will go wrong this year." Michael lived on a mixture of hard work and optimism. "If we haven't cleared the stall by lunch-time, I'll send Guy home with the van, and come on by bus later."

"Try to be home for lunch," Alicia urged.

"I'll get a snack if I can't."

"I know your snacks," Alicia said scornfully. "Two tomatoes and a lettuce."

She was glad to be able to send him off with a laugh. Guy came rushing, to wash his hands, give her a peck of a kiss, and then take a running leap up to the seat next to his father. Neither of them appeared to have noticed that Alicia was troubled. She closed and locked the box, and put it in a drawer, which she also locked. Two or three accounts had to be met in cash today, so they wouldn't bank any money until to-morrow. She went out of the office to the bungalow close by it, large, and well proportioned; it had been attractively and solidly built between the wars. The kitchen where the daily, Mrs. Glee, was working over-looked the grounds and the small office, and anyone who stepped into the office also stepped on to a bell-push hidden under a mat, warning anyone in the house.

That was how Alicia could be so sure that only the family had been, this morning.

Mrs. Glee, a diminutive countrywoman with a townswoman's brusqueness, greeted her almost sharply.

"Morning, Mrs. Vane. They've got off early this morning."

"Yes, it's not yet ten o'clock," Alicia answered.

"Good thing some of the family believes in punc-tuality," declared Mrs. Glee.

MISSING MONEY

Alicia was so full of thoughts about Hester that the remark didn't at first sink in; she was at the door, on her way up to the bedroom, when it did. She stopped.

"What did you say?"

"Oh, it's no business of mine," said Mrs. Glee, "but if your Hester doesn't come back one day and tell you she's got the sack, I shall be surprised."

The chill which was already in Alicia's mind seemed to become icy.

"What on earth makes you say that?"

"Well she's due at the shop at half-past nine, to my knowledge, and at half-past nine most Fridays I see her talking to a man friend with a flash sports car. Once now and again is all right, but *every* Friday's coming it, I should think. It's none of my business, but if anyone told me that about my daughter, I'd regard it as a favour."

Mrs. Glee made no doubt that she regarded this as a favour, too.

"Yes," said Alicia. "I'm glad you told me, Mrs. Glee. Are you sure it's every Friday?"

"Positive."

"Is it always the same man?"

"Certain sure," declared Mrs. Glee, "and I don't think I'd be very happy if he was meeting my daughter regularly, either."

If Alicia asked "why not" it would turn all this into kitchen scandal; the difficulty was to forbear comment without annoying the other woman. A car slowed down outside, and was almost certainly the village store van, coming to collect tomatoes and lettuce. The engine stopped.

"I must go," said Alicia, and took the chance to hurry out.

As she handed the vanman the baskets of tomatoes and the boxes of lettuce, took the money and gave him his receipted bill, she was thinking: "It's on Fridays that I miss the money." Was it possible that Hester was making regular payments to this man? Alicia wished that she had asked more about the man, and why Mrs. Glee did not like him, but it would be impossible to re-open the subject and Mrs. Glee was not likely to broach it again. She had done her duty, and would let it rest.

"And here are the papers," the vanman said.

"Thank you, Jack."

"It's a pleasure," the elderly man assured her. "Well, I must be off, I've a special for delivery at the Hall this morning, mustn't keep them waiting. Did you see that Rolls-Bentley which purred past last night—maroon and silver grey. What a beauty!" At seventy-one, Jack's enthusiasm for cars was at least as great as Guy's.

"It would be Mr. Mannering's, I expect."

"Mr. Who?"

"Mr. Mannering. You know, John Mannering."

"I don't think I do know." Alicia was thinking of Hester again, and the man in the flashy sports car.

"Well, it's in the *Gazette*," Jack said. "He's come down to advise on refurnishing some of the old rooms at the Hall. He's a famous antique dealer—you'll know him when you read about it. His wife's coming later—the painter, *you* know."

"Oh, yes, of course," Alicia said, to save trouble.

In fact, the new Mannering meant nothing in spite of the *aides-memoires* of an antique dealer and a wife who painted. Alicia was not even slightly interested in any visitors at the Hall whether they had a Rolls-Bentley or not. Only Hester mattered. As she began to make the beds, she realised that it would be impossible to tell Michael at this stage; she must try to find out what was happening, and to put it right herself. The difficulty would be having a talk with Hester without one of the others being present; they were always liable to come in unexpectedly.

She could go into Gilston and have lunch with Hester; or better, go in during the afternoon and have tea with her. They could talk freely if they went to Madden's, with its separate stalls for luncheon or tea. The decision made, Alicia felt some sense of relief, bustled more, and even managed to tell herself that she was probably making much out of nothing. She went out to pick some wallflowers and tulips for the afternoon market, leaving Mrs. Glee to look after the lunch. Michael wasn't likely to be home for lunch, of course.

In a way, she hoped that he wouldn't.

The van came swinging into the drive, Guy driving and by himself. She heard him whistling as he dumped the empty boxes, and then came towards the kitchen, greeted Mrs. Glee, and washed sketchily—he liked washing little more today than he had five years ago.

Then he came in breezily.

"Hallo, Mum, had a good morning? Nice lot of tulips I see, but the wallflowers are looking a bit tatty." He sat on the arm of a chair, tall, lean, healthy-looking; happy and for some reason excited. "Has the *Gazette* arrived?"

"You're almost sitting on it."

"I never think to look under *The Times*," Guy said, and picked up the local newspaper and shook it open. "Anything in about John Mannering, I wonder. I saw his car this morning—wooosh! Loveliest thing on four wheels you ever saw."

"Really?"

"He was browsing among the old junk stalls, amazing how a man like that can't keep away from old stuff, isn't it? Did you read how he found a Van Gogh on a junk stall down in Devon, bought it for thirty bob, and sold it for nine thousand pounds."

That really startled his mother.

"If that's the kind of thing he does I don't want to hear about him," she said, partly to see how Guy would react.

He grinned at her.

"Old stick-in-the-mud, that's what you are. I don't

believe you ever read anything except the woman's page and what the stars don't foretell. Mannering split the proceeds with the old boy who owned the shop he'd bought it from, on condition that the old boy split his share with the old lady who'd sold it to him with a lot of other junk. That, my dear mother, is the kind of man John Mannering is."

Alicia laughed. "All right, I apologise to him."

"So I should think! I'd love a chance to meet him, I wonder if—hallo, here's a big article and a photograph of him and his wife! She's the artist." Guy brought the *Gilston Gazette* to his mother, and she saw a remarkably good-looking, smiling man of about forty, and an equally handsome woman who seemed a little too severe. The caption beneath the picture read:

> Mr. and Mrs. John Mannering, the famous private detective and antique dealer and his wife, are to be guests at Norton Hall, where he will advise Lord Norton on various matters pertaining to his collection of antiques and old masters. Mrs. Mannering is the eminent portrait painter.

"How about that?" Guy asked, "I wonder if he is there to give advice on whether there's any funny business going on at Norton Hall. I once heard that Mannering does most of his snooping in the guise of a dealer. He must be good, even Scotland Yard consults him. I—ah, food!" His eyes glistened. "Stew with dumplings, that's just about right for me. Save a plateful for Dad, I'll bet he'll be ravenous when he gets home."

"I'll see that he doesn't starve," Alicia assured him.

"I bet you will," said Guy, and then looked up and asked unexpectedly: "Mum, what's the matter with Hester this last few weeks? Is she going through another ordeal by young love?"

Alicia said, as off-handedly as she could: "I haven't noticed anything. Why?"

"And they say the maternal instinct never lets you down," scoffed Guy. "She's moping about the dickens of a lot. I saw her in town this morning, and she looked washed out, almost as if she hadn't slept. She was bright enough this morning, wasn't she?"

"I thought so," Alicia said. "I'll keep an eye on her, you eat your lunch."

CHAPTER TWO

UNTRUTHFUL DAUGHTER

"But, Mother," Hester insisted, "there's nothing the matter with me, nothing at all. I've a bit of a headache today, that's all."

Alicia said: "Hester, you ought to know by now that it's no use lying to me."

She saw the blood rush to Hester's cheeks, and the flood of anger which made daughter so much like father; Guy took after her, Alicia, and seldom lost his temper. Hester bunched her hands on the table, and for a moment it looked as if she would jump up and walk out. She managed to restrain herself, although when she spoke her voice was tense and angry.

"I'm not lying, and I resent that."

"Hester," Alicia said, trying to be matter-of-fact, "you and I needn't keep secrets from each other. We haven't so far, or I think we haven't. And if I know what the trouble is I may be able to help."

"Mother, for the last time, there isn't any trouble."

Alicia said: "All right, dear, if that's how you want it to be, I'll say no more—on one condition."

Hester's green-gold eyes were still flashing with anger.

"I don't think you've any right to make conditions."

"I think I have with this," Alicia said, keeping her voice low and looking straight into her daughter's eyes. "I'll say no more about it provided you repay the twenty pounds you've borrowed from the office."

She had confronted Hester—always the unpredictable member of the family—with challenges like this for many years. The outburst of temper, the flashing eyes, the pallor—these were all familiar and in their way precious; would the next move be familiar, too? The coming of tears which never fell, a flush, and a sudden burst of contrition.

Alicia almost prayed that it would.

But if the usual reaction were to come, it was taking a long time. The shock effect was there, and Alicia had no doubt at all of Hester's guilt. The word, actually in her mind, had an ugly sound. She saw the tension in Hester's eyes, waiting for the moment of breaking down, and saw instead that her daughter's lips tightened. For a moment she thought that Hester was going to deny the theft; so for a moment she looked ahead at dangerous, different days.

Then Hester said stiffly: "I'm sorry, I can't discuss it."

"You'll have to, Hester."

"Well, I can't."

"There must be a good reason."

"I can't discuss it," Hester said, she picked up her handbag, lying on the carved oak table between them. "I'm sorry." She stood up, hesitated, and then asked in a moment of desperation which was more like the childhood Hester: "Does Dad know about this?"

Alicia hesitated before she said very carefully:

"Not yet. And he won't, provided——"

Hester turned, pushed between the table and the seat behind her, and started to walk towards the head of the stairs. Her coat caught on a cup, which toppled and began to fall. In a flurry of movement the girl saved it, righted it on its saucer and, biting her lips and avoiding Alicia's eyes, strode out of the café.

"How can I make her talk?" Alicia asked herself. "If the idea of Michael knowing doesn't frighten her, what will?"

There were so many more questions forcing themselves upon her mind. Why had Hester taken the money? Why did she harden herself? Why did she refuse to talk about it? What kind of trouble was she in? Guy had seen it, Michael would soon, and once that happened there would be no way of keeping the truth from him. Almost with a sense of shock, Alicia knew that the last thing she wanted was to tell Michael.

Had she handled this badly?

The cup of tea had been pleasant; and both of them had pretended that all had been well, but in fact Hester had realised almost from the start that her mother had some special purpose in suggesting tea together. Hester, mannequin at Cobham's, the one departmental store in Gilston, was always allowed half an hour for tea and unless there were special displays, could always stretch that to three-quarters of an hour. She had, today.

A waitress came up, bright and pert.

"Did you enjoy your tea?"

"Yes, thank you." Alicia paid, tipped, gathered up her own belongings, and went downstairs. The small café, full of oak beams, had once been part of an inn, and later a chop-house. The wood that she touched was nearly four hundred years old. She wasn't thinking about the antiquity of the building, until she heard a woman say:

"I think it's about the same age as Quinns, Mr. Mannering!"

The name made her glance into the main restaurant room, on the ground floor. Oak rafters, a great inglenook fireplace, some beautiful brasses and copper cooking utensils met the eye, and standing in the middle of the hearth a man she recognised immediately as the John Mannering who had so impressed Guy.

He was even better-looking in person than his photograph suggested; he was smiling, and talking to the middle-aged woman who owned the restaurant. He glanced up, as if his gaze were drawn by Alicia's, and looked straight at her. He gave a little smile, which seemed to light up the whole of his face.

UNTRUTHFUL DAUGHTER 19

Alicia turned away, and hurried out.

Along the wide High Street, with space for parking in the middle, was the immaculate maroon and silver Rolls-Bentley—a car for which Guy thought he would give his right arm. There it stood, representing three or four years profit from Michael's work. Why should one man find life so easy, another so difficult? Alicia felt so bitter that she forgot for the moment that Michael enjoyed his work, and would rather scrape by at the market garden than make a fortune while living in a city.

The real trouble was Hester, of course.

It would be difficult for Hester to come home and face her now; that was always the trouble when a situation went wrong. Again Alicia tried to tell herself that she had handled the situation well, and wasn't to blame; yet by the time she was at the bus stop, she was blaming herself. It was a little after five. Most of the stall-holders were packing up. The large stretch of the High Street set aside for the smaller growers to sell produce from their gardens—the section where Michael and Guy sold—was empty. There was a long queue for the bus, and Alicia wondered whether she would be able to get on the first which came along. Then a scarlet sports car flashed by, with a middle-aged, grey-haired man at the wheel. Alicia jumped to the possibility that it was the flashy car driven by the man whom Hester saw on Fridays.

Alicia had caught only a glimpse of the man, tried to remember what he looked like, and could remember only his grey hair and duffle coat, a rather reckless air about him. Then the bus came up, the twenty or thirty people waiting shuffled along; when Alicia was four away from the head of the queue, the conductress said:

"Next bus, please."

That meant another twenty minutes' wait.

No one complained as the bus drove off. A moment or two later, the luxurious Rolls-Bentley came by, with

Mannering at the wheel; otherwise the car was empty. To go to the Hall, he would have to pass the bungalow. The driver glanced at Alicia, and felt sure that he recognised her, then he went on, and that unreasoning bitterness welled up. She was staring after the Rolls-Bentley when a van stopped, and Guy called:

"Like a lift, lady?"

"Guy!"

"Brought in a special load, Dad told me to keep an eye open for you," Guy said, leaning across and opening the door. "All right, I'll close it." It was a relief to sit down. "How did the tea party go?"

"Tea party?" Alicia was startled.

"I bumped into Peg, and she said you and Hester were having a heart-to-heart at Madden's I've a feeling you were pulling the wool over my eyes when you said you hadn't noticed anything wrong with Sis."

"Don't be absurd, Guy."

"All right, keep it to yourself," conceded Guy. They were already out of the town, and the bungalow and Vane's Market Garden was four miles away on the main London road. "I had a bit of the real luck, by the way."

"That's good."

"Practically got run over by John Mannering's car."

"Guy!"

"How about that for luck?"

"A man has no right to go racing about in a car like that, as if he owned the town."

"Here, steady," Guy protested, laughing. "It was my fault, I was gaping at the Bentley so goof-eyed that I didn't notice Mannering was going to reverse. Funny thing, I don't know whether you see what I do, but there's a picturesque look about him. Bit of the old Elizabethan, if you know what I mean."

"I think you're being absurd," Alicia said.

"That man stands head and shoulders above the average, take it from me," Guy declared. "One glimpse was enough to show that everything people say about him is right."

He went on talking, partly about Mannering, his detective work and his reputation with Scotland Yard, and partly about the day's business; then about the possibility of buying the farm next year. He knew—as the whole family knew—that if it were to be bought, they would need three thousand pounds in ready money: the rest could stay on mortgage. Until a few days ago, Alicia had taken it for granted that every one of the family wanted it for Michael nearly as much as he wanted it for himself.

But not Hester, apparently.

"Hallo, Ally," Michael said, about half-past six. It was still broad daylight and Guy was in the garden; digging. Michael limped in, took off his hat and hung it behind the office door, and dropped down on the desk. "I'm tired today, for some reason. You look a bit peaky, too."

"I'm all right, but you work too hard."

"There's no such thing," retorted Michael. "Hester home yet?"

"No."

"She's late, isn't she?"

"I suppose she is," agreed Alicia.

"Noticed anything about her lately?"

Alicia said, slowly, almost painfully: "Why, have you?"

"She hasn't been her usual self," answered Michael, and ran his fingers through that thick grey hair. "Been a bit snappy at times, too, I nearly told her off about it last night. That time when she wanted the television off, and Guy wanted it on."

"Oh, all young people get edgy," Alicia said.

"Sure that's all?"

"What else would you think?" Alicia made herself ask, just as she made herself smile at him. "There may be a boy friend and true love probably isn't running true. She hasn't confided in me this time, but she will if it becomes really serious."

"Ah, yes," said Michael, and his face lit up. It was a rugged face, and he was bronzed by a winter and spring in the open air, and his grey eyes were very clear. "You'll keep an eye on her, won't you?" he went on. "I should hate her to run into any trouble. Ever since she began to grow up I've been a bit scared." He gave a laugh which didn't ring true. "Silly, isn't it?"

"Of course I'll watch her, Micky," Alicia assured him. "She'll be all right."

"I don't mind admitting that in one way I'll be glad when she really falls in love and looks as if she'll settle down," Michael declared. "I almost dread her coming and telling us that she's going to have a baby. There's a hell of a lot of that about these days. It couldn't happen to our Hester, could it?"

Alicia felt as if she could scream; but she managed to make her eyes twinkle, and to say mildly.

"Biologically, I hope it could. In practice——"

Michael's responding laugh had much less strain in it.

"Bless you! Well, believe it or not I'm going to take the rest of the day off. What's good for supper?"

"Ham and salad," declared Alicia.

"Why do you buy this rabbit's food?" He grinned and went off, whistling under his breath, and she believed that she had completely dispersed his anxiety over the kind of presentiment he had about Hester. Probably every father felt the same. He was hypersensitive, and always had been about Hester. If he discovered anything seriously wrong it would hurt him desperately.

There couldn't be. Could there?

Alicia thought: "I wish she would come home."

She sensed the strain and the anxiety in Michael's

UNTRUTHFUL DAUGHTER

mind when, two hours later, there was no sign of Hester. Every now and again, he went to the front door and looked out, but it was a nervous reaction, he did not really expect to see her. It was quite dark. Guy had gone to a sports club for table tennis and billiards, and would probably be back about eleven o'clock. Hester was never out for supper unless she had told her parents she was going to be; and if anything did make her late, she always telephoned.

The figures on the television screen danced but made no sense. Alicia kept seeing Hester's face, when she had jumped up from the tea-table, and when she had turned to ask if her father knew about the missing money. The torment was twofold, now; she blamed and reproached herself for mishandling the situation, and she hardly knew how to tell Michael. He would have to be told something, soon, and there was no sense in lying. Silence didn't matter so much, but if she told a positive lie it would break the trust between them.

He was pretending to read *The Times*, and Alicia knew that he had one ear open for the sound of footsteps. A man walked along outside, the sound faded, and then came a rustling of the newspaper, Alicia pretended that she hadn't noticed.

"I'm going to call Ted Hennessy," Michael said, suddenly. "Hester must have met with an accident, she's never been late like this before."

He jumped up, and stepped towards the telephone which was in a corner by the front window. In this mood he would do exactly what he said, without thinking twice. Hennessy was an old friend of his, and an inspector in the county police force—actually in the criminal investigation department. Alicia knew him well, and knew his wife Muriel even better.

She jumped up.

"Mike, don't make a fuss."

"Good God, I've been as calm as a badger!"

"You'll only feel a fool if you start the police making inquiries and she turns up."

"I don't mind being made a fool for that," Michael said gruffly, and lifted the telephone and began to dial. He watched Alicia as he did so, and she was almost frantic, for she knew that the truth could not now be long delayed. She needed a kind of miracle; the telephone to ring and Hester to explain, or Hester to come hurrying. Hester. . . .

"Ally, what's the matter?" Michael asked, in a quiet, tense voice. He put the receiver down, but was looking at her so oddly that she did not feel relief. He stood by the telephone staring at her. "Tell me what's happening," he ordered. "Something odd's going on with Hester, I've sensed it for weeks. Why don't you tell me?"

"Mike, I——" she broke off.

"I don't know whether you expect me to become the Victorian father or not, but I assure you I can take whatever's coming," Michael assured her, and he managed one of his rather fierce smiles. "What has happened? What kind of trouble is she in?"

"Mike," Alicia said, "I don't know, I only wish I did." This was the moment, and he had to be told. Now that she was about to start she hoped that neither of the children would come in and interrupt.

CHAPTER THREE

PROUD PARENT

You could live with a man for over twenty years, Alicia told herself, and still not be really sure how he would react to any unusual situation. She had hated the thought of telling Michael about the missing money, but now he knew—and had practically ignored it. He stood looking at her, frowning, almost like a stranger; and she knew that he wasn't really thinking of her.

"One thing's certain, she wouldn't have taken the money without a damned good reason," he said. "Do you know anything about a man friend?"

"No."

"She usually confides in you if there's one on the end of a string, doesn't she?"

"Yes," Alicia said and added: "Always." Then for some ridiculous reason she felt like bursting into tears. She dropped to the arm of a chair and put her hands in front of her face. "I hoped she always would," she went on, huskily. "Mike, what have I done wrong? Where have I failed?"

His brisk voice was a welcome douche of cold water.

"Don't dramatise it, sweet. You haven't failed any of us. Good Lord, there's no need for you to *cry*." He came towards her, and put an arm round her shoulder; there was comfort in his nearness. "I quite see why you preferred not to tell me, if it were any ordinary thing Hester would have cleared it up with you. There's one thing I'm sure of—it isn't plain dishonesty. Not in one of our children."

Of course, Alicia thought, she should have realised that he would take that view; would find a kind of excuse if not a justification for Hester, and she was glad that he had; fiercely glad. The pallor in Hester's cheeks and the glitter in her eyes suggested that he was right.

"Did she say she wouldn't come home?"

"No," Alicia answered. "I knew she might find it difficult to face me, but——"

"Not like Hester to refuse to face something unpleasant," Michael said, and Alicia found herself wondering how right he was, and whether he was fooling himself. "She wouldn't have gone along to the club, would she?"

"She doesn't, often."

"No, not since she stopped enjoying table tennis," Michael said. "I think we ought to telephone a few of her friends, and ask if they've seen her. We can explain that we're worried."

"What about Ted Hennessy?"

Michael looked astonishingly like Guy when he grinned, as he did now.

"I knew that if I threatened to talk to Ted you'd tell me what was on your mind. I know you can read me like a book but it cuts the other way sometimes! Now, where would she be likely to stay if she's sulking?"

Alicia could have kissed him for his common sense.

"She might possibly be at Marion Harrison's, or at Aunt Bee's, or——"

"You think up the places and jot down the telephone numbers, and I'll call them," Michael said, and strode to the telephone. "Aunt Bee's is Gilston 151, I'll start with her."

Watching him as he picked up the receiver and dialled briskly, Alicia felt that she had never loved him so much or understood him so well. He was determined not to let her see how worried he was, but beneath this briskness there was a deep and growing anxiety. The effect of knowing about the money had not yet caught up with him; his first reaction was to be sure that there was a reasonable explanation. Now he actually winked at her; but when he looked at the window, where the curtain was drawn back so that they could see into the street, she saw the way his jaws were working.

"Hallo, Aunt Bee," he greeted with forced heartiness. "Yes, fine, thanks. . . . Yes. . . . Oh, I am sorry." He was grimacing at Alicia now. "Well, yes, we're a little worried about Hester, she isn't home yet and we wondered if she'd left a message for us which didn't come through. . . . She's not with you? . . . No, of course not, I'm sure there's no need to worry."

At last, he was able to ring off.

He dialled as Alicia called out the next number.

"Hallo, Mrs. Harrison. . . . Yes, fine, thanks. . . . Oh, that's good; we're having a very good yield this year, too . . . well I'd certainly like to think they're the best tomatoes in the district. . . . We wondered if Hester. . . ."

In all, he made five calls; after each, his tension and Alicia's grew. It was now a quarter to eleven. That wasn't late. It was ridiculous to think that it was late, but this kind of thing had never happened before.

Michael replaced the receiver slowly.

"I don't like it," he said. "She can't have run away, can she? Ally, don't misunderstand me, but what kind of a row did you have with her?"

"It wasn't really a row."

"Exactly what did you say?"

"I've told you," Alicia said.

It was strange how emotions could vary, minute by minute. Of course, he did not blame her with his mind and whatever happened he would not; but emotionally he was beginning to wonder whether she could have prevented this; whether it was her fault in any way. All the evening she had been asking herself the same question, but now that it was in his mind, she resented it. The reassurance he had given her was gone, and it was the kind of comfort she needed badly.

A light appeared in the roadway, and the beam of a lamp turned towards the bungalow and shone on the window for a moment, then vanished.

"That's Guy," Michael said. "Do you think Hester would confide in him?"

"He might have a message," Alicia said, and jumped up. They went together into the kitchen, where Guy would come. Michael squeezed Alicia's hand, but it was a considered gesture, not spontaneous. He was frightened, of course; as she was. They put on the light as they heard Guy slamming the office door; he always kept his bicycle in there at night. He came hurrying, not whistling. Usually he whistled gaily to announce his coming, and anything that was even slightly out of the ordinary tonight seemed to hold a special significance.

Michael opened the door as he approached, and the kitchen light fell on his bright eyes and eager face.

"Hallo, Dad!"

"Hallo, Guy. Have you——"

"Gosh, what a night!" Guy interrupted, as if he hadn't heard his father's comment. "You'd never believe it—I've been questioned by the police."

Michael exclaimed: "*What?*" in a voice which startled Guy; and Alicia felt as if someone was clutching her with cold hands.

"Damn it, *I'm* not under suspicion," Guy said, staring at them in bewilderment. "Sorry if I scared you."

"It's all right, Guy," Alicia said.

"We're a bit worried because Hester isn't home," Michael reported.

"Isn't she?" Guy asked almost carelessly; obviously he couldn't keep his mind on a minor domestic problem. "It was terrific. A chap was killed sitting in his car."

Alicia winced.

"Where?" asked Michael.

Alicia wanted to cry: *What car? What man?*

"As a matter of fact, just inside the grounds of the Hall, in that copse—you know," Guy went on, and his parents had never seen him more excited. "Heaven knows what he was doing there, unless he was with a girl. You know." Guy was young and naïve enough to glance at his mother as if she would be shocked. "Anyhow, he's as dead as a doornail. I didn't actually see him, but I did see the sheet covering the body as they put him into an ambulance. There must be twenty policemen down at the Hall Gates." He gave an explosive little laugh. "It won't be long before Mannering's on the spot, I'll bet."

What car? Alicia wanted to scream.

"What did the police want with you?" Michael asked. It was clear that he was forcing himself to be calm, that he wondered if there was any association between this and the fact that Hester was missing. But he did not know of Mrs. Glee's gossip; he did not know of the man with whom Hester talked every Friday morning; the theft mornings.

"Oh, I'd cycled past on the way to the club and they wanted to know if I'd seen anything, that's all," Guy answered. "I wish I had, it would really be something to be witness in a case like that, and if Mannering does get called in, he'd make a beeline for me. No such luck! Mum, can I make myself a welsh rarebit?"

"Guy," Alicia began, and stopped, making both husband and son turn to look at her intently. She knew that she had lost colour, and they would hardly fail to notice it. "Guy, what was the car like?"

"Eh?"

"What was the car like?"

"The one this man was murdered in," Michael explained.

"Oh, a little sports model. Not a bad jalopy at all. I've seen it about several times. Saw it today, as a matter of fact, and the police wanted to know if I got a good look at the driver."

Alicia didn't speak. Michael glanced at her, obviously puzzled and more worried.

"Did you?" Michael asked.

"Well, fair, but you know how it is when you're interested in a car, you don't take much notice of the driver unless she happens to be young and pretty." He grinned and turned towards the larder. "Grey-haired chap about forty-five, I suppose. Oldish, anyhow."

Oldish.

"You get what you want to eat, and come into the living-room when you've finished," Michael said.

"Right-ho. I say, Mum, what's the matter?"

He could be such a boy.

"I'm a bit over-tired," Alicia answered, and was glad that she could turn away, cross the hall and go into the sitting-room. She wanted to sit down. Michael went straight to the corner cupboard where they kept their small store of wines and spirits, took out a whisky bottle and a syphon, and mixed her a drink. He didn't speak until he handed it to her. She drank. He hadn't put in much soda, and it made her gasp.

After a moment or two, he asked:

"What is it? Alicia?"

She told him.

He looked at her intently, and she could tell what thoughts were passing through his mind; knew that he shared the horror of what this might imply. This was the man whom Hester had seen, of course—and he might have been with a girl just before he had been murdered.

Suddenly, the door opened wider, and Guy came in.

"I don't know what's going on but I mean to," he said. "What is it, Dad? Hester's all right, isn't she?" When neither of them answered, he went on more sharply. "For heaven's sake don't just stand there looking at me as if I'm a little boy. I'm grown up. Remember me? What's scaring you like this?"

"It's all right, Guy," Michael said. "We're probably

making a lot of fuss about nothing. But Hester's not back, and we've discovered that she'd been seeing rather a lot of a middle-aged man who runs a sports car."

Guy actually backed away from them.

"Hester can't have been with him tonight," Alicia said, sharply. "It's impossible, she couldn't have been."

"I know one thing, I'm going to find out," declared Guy grimly. "Mr. Hennessy was down at the Hall gates. If he knows anything about Hester, he'd tell us." Guy seemed to have matured several years in a few seconds. "And it's no use saying you'll go, Dad, they'd wonder what was worrying you, but they won't be surprised that curiosity took me back. I——"

He broke off, for a car sounded outside, the engine very loud; and then the headlights shone past the window, and the car slowed down. A moment later a man got out, and in the light of the street lamp they all recognised Ted Hennessy.

CHAPTER FOUR

UGLY FACTS

"I'll talk to Ted," Michael said, commandingly. "Ally, you go into the kitchen with Guy, and get him some supper—Ted won't be surprised if I see him alone." He gave Alicia no time to argue, but hustled them both into the kitchen. All the time, footsteps sounded on the approach to the front door. That was unusual; Ted Hennessy, the family friend, usually came round to the back door. There were two sets of footsteps. Alicia actually went to the gas stove, where the grill was glowing red; and then as the front door bell rang, she swung round and went back to the hall.

"It's no use, Mike, I can't stay there. I've got to know what's happened."

"We don't want Ted to think——"

"He'll soon know that we're worried, and it won't help to pretend we're not."

Michael might try to insist, but he hadn't much time, and certainly couldn't raise his voice, for the two men at the front door would hear anything above a normal speaking tone. There was a moment's hesitation, before Michael seemed to relax, and said:

"You're right, I'm sorry. What about Guy?"

"I think he ought to be in on this, too."

"All right, get him."

Alicia hurried into the kitchen as Michael went to open the front door. The kitchen door was wide open, and a cold wind cut in. The light was on in the office. Alicia hurried to the back step as Guy appeared, hat on, wheeling his racing bicycle.

"I'm going to poke around and see what I can find out," he said. "I know two of the policemen who're down there, they're in the soccer team. I can probably get them to tell me more than Mr. Hennessy will tell Dad. Don't worry." He cocked a leg over his bicycle and waved to his mother. She did not try to stop him, but went back into the house. She hesitated by the door of the kitchen, closed it, and then went into the living-room.

Hennessy was a big man, much more massive than Michael, a countryman with a slow, deliberate voice, blue eyes, a kind of solidity which seemed to come only from the country. He wore a heavy belted coat and carried a trilby hat; as always, he looked immaculate, for his wife made sure that he was the best-dressed policeman in Gilston. With him was a smaller grey-clad man, whom Alicia had seen about in the town; a sharp-featured man whom she disliked on sight.

"Hallo, Ted," she greeted.

"Hallo, Alicia." He came forward and shook hands. "This is Detective Sergeant Winterton."

Alicia said: "How are you?"

"Evening, ma'am," Winterton responded more in the tone of an anxious-to-please shopkeeper than a policeman investigating a serious crime.

"What's the matter?" Alicia asked.

"I've just been telling Mike that there may be nothing to this," Hennessy said, "but I don't mind admitting I'm sorry to hear that Hester's not been home this evening." He was very blunt; as she had expected, and he did not look away from her. Winterton stood by the door, giving the absurd impression that he meant to make sure that she didn't go out. "I gather Guy's told you about the murder?"

"It can't have anything to do with Hester," Alicia said, and the words sounded hollow even in her own ears.

"Last thing I'd expect," Hennessy agreed, and Alicia noticed that he did not really commit himself very far. He had never seemed so broad-shouldered, and to her had never seemed so formal. "The fact is,

Alicia, that the dead man is known to have been with a young woman earlier this evening, and they were heard quarrelling. The young woman wasn't seen clearly, but the man was. It's known that he drove away with the young woman, and they were seen near the spot where the man was found at about half-past nine. The man was found at about a quarter-past ten, with a knife wound in his neck."

Alicia found herself echoing: "A knife wound."

"Yes." Hennessey went on quickly, as if glad that this part of his duty was past. "Of course there's not the slightest reason to assume that the young woman was Hester."

He stopped.

Winterton shuffled his feet a little.

Michael asked quietly: "Then why did you come straight to us, Ted?"

"We have to examine every aspect," Hennessy answered; he was now being almost absurdly formal. "I was very anxious to establish the fact that Hester hadn't been out this evening. If she'd been at home, then——"

"For goodness' sake tell us what brought you?" exclaimed Alicia.

Hennessy looked uneasy and embarrassed.

"All right, I won't beat about the bush," he said. "Hester's been seen with this man on several occasions. She was seen talking to him this morning, on her way to work. What was she wearing when she went this morning?"

"Her green duffle coat and scarf."

"Hm, yes," said Hennessey, and looked even more ill-at-ease. "The witness who saw the man and the young woman together said that the woman was wearing a green or blue duffle-coat. H'm." He was now acutely embarrassed, which wasn't surprising, for—the finger of suspicion seemed to be pointing straight at Hester. "I had a quick check made, and found that Hester's motor-scooter is parked in the market place, where it's been all day. She hasn't been home, has she?"

Alicia snapped: "Of course she hasn't!"

Michael said: "No, Ted, she hasn't. Don't make the situation any worse."

"Sorry," mumbled Hennessy, "but it wouldn't be surprising if a mother and father tried to shelter their daughter if she was in trouble."

"We'd do that all right," Michael assured him.

"Sure you would—and why not?" Hennessy glanced at Winterton, and all the time Alicia was aware of the thin-faced sergeant standing there and looking at her, and still on unofficial guard at the door. "Mike, don't misunderstand me when I say this: if Hester comes back, let us know at once. Don't try to hide her, or anything like that. It would only make the situation worse."

"Ted, do you seriously mean to suggest that you think our Hester could be involved in a crime like this?" Alicia heard herself asking. They were only words but difficult to utter; and riding over her distress and anxiety there was anger with Ted—with the family friend who could behave like this. "It's absolutely ludicrous."

"Ted knows it is," Michael said.

"He isn't behaving as if he thinks that."

"Ally, don't take this wrong," Hennessy begged, almost pleadingly. "I've got a job to do. I don't know what's happened—I can only tell you what I know. The man was seen with Hester today, and he's been killed in a way which a woman could do. I've got to sift the facts, that's all. I don't for a moment believe that Hester is involved, but I've got to find her and talk to her. I've been put in charge of the case, and if we can solve it quickly it will be better for all concerned. All I'm asking is that you let us know at once if Hester gets in touch with you, or when she comes home."

"We will," Michael promised.

"That's all that matters," Hennessy said. He gulped, and added: "I hate worrying Ally."

"You seem to relish it," Alicia said icily.

"Confound it, Ally——"

"Excuse me, sir," said Winterton, speaking for the first time since he had greeted Alicia, "but you asked me to remind you to inquire whether Miss Vane had told her parents about her association with the deceased."

Alicia swung round on him, angrily, might have snapped at him had Michael not gripped her arm. She knew that he was right to restrain her and that she was behaving badly. Deep down, she knew the reason: she was terrified of the picture drawn by these ugly facts.

"Did Hester know a middle-aged man who owned a sports car?" Hennessy asked.

"Not to my knowledge," said Michael.

"Did she talk about a middle-aged acquaintance?"

"No."

"Was she having a—er—a romance?" Alicia was sure Hennessy had been going to say: " . . . having an affair?"

"Was she, darling?" Michael turned and asked.

"Not that I know of, but she didn't tell me about every time she and a boy held hands."

"Has she been herself lately?"

"Of course."

"How do you mean, Ted?" Michael was fighting hard to keep this as informal and as unhurtful as he could. He still held Alicia's hand tightly, warning her not to lose her head.

"I mean, has she been worried, or stayed out later than usual at night, or been more secretive, short of money, anything like that."

"I don't think so," Michael said. "Has she, darling?"

Aliaia answered tartly: "No."

"Any reason why you should think so?" demanded Michael.

Hennessy hesitated, looked at Winterton, obviously wishing that the sergeant wasn't here, and then said that there was no special reason, he just wanted to know. He hesitated before moving towards the door, having to pass Alicia on the way. He started to speak, but stopped himself, made a helpless and rather touching little gesture, and then went out. Detective Sergeant Winterton had already opened the door, and Michael was going along the passage with them when the telephone bell rang.

Alicia caught her breath.

Michael swung round, but suddenly she realised that she was nearest the telephone, and that she could answer it first. She almost ran across the room and snatched up the receiver, and then she saw Michael just inside the room and the two policemen in the doorway, looking rather as if each wanted to get in ahead of the other.

"Hallo," Alicia said, tautly. "Hallo—hallo, there. Hester, is that you?"

She heard nothing.

"*Hester, is that you?*"

Then she heard a sound like the pressing of a button at a prepayment call box, and she waited, her expression keeping Michael and the other men away.

CHAPTER FIVE

GUY

Any moment, Alicia felt sure, she would hear Hester's voice. She took it for granted that it would be her daughter, and was telling herself that she must speak calmly, must not do anything to alarm or worry her; somehow, she had to help—and the best chance was now.

Then, *Guy* spoke.

"That you, Mum?"

"Guy!"

Michael relaxed, and she saw him put a hand to his forehead.

"Mum, is that——"

"Yes, of course it's me. Guy, where are you? I don't want you to stay out, I want——"

"I thought I'd better call because I think I'm going to be late and I didn't want to cause another scare," Guy said. "Is Dad there?"

"You can tell me anything you can tell him. Guy, have you seen Hester?"

"I wish I had," Guy said fervently. "Mum, let me speak to Dad."

She could have shouted at him: but it would do no good, and might make the situation worse. What had she done, to have brought this on herself? Why had she talked to Hester like she had this afternoon?

Michael, by her side, took the receiver without a word to her, and said:

"Hallo, Guy. What is it?"

He seemed to listen for an age, and then the last thing Alicia had expected happened; he gave a little smile, actually had to stifle a laugh. He soon sobered, and glanced at Hennessy and Winterton, almost warily. Then he said:

"Well, it won't do any harm. Be careful, Guy. . . . If you're going to be in too late, telephone us again. We won't go to bed until we hear."

He rang off.

"Mike, what did he say?" Hennessy demanded, almost too quickly. There was a pleading note in his voice, asking that his friend should not hold out on him. Winterton had a crafty look, and there was a glitter in his eyes which suggested a kind of gloating.

Alicia felt that she hated Winterton.

Michael spread his hands, and smiled wryly.

"Guy's been told pretty much the same story that you told us," he said, "and he seems to think that the police do believe that Hester was involved in this. So he's going up to the Hall to ask John Mannering if he'll help to prove that the police are wrong."

"John Man——" Hennessy began, and then broke into a grin. Winterton looked down his nose, as if he didn't like the news at all. "Oh, well, that can't do any harm, and it might even help," Hennessy went on. "I wonder what put that idea into Guy's head."

"Don't see that it matters," Michael said. He slid an arm round Alicia's waist, hugged her, and at the same time looked very straightly at Hennessy. "Ted, why aren't you being frank with us? You think the evidence points straight at Hester, don't you?"

Hennessy didn't answer; and that was answer enough.

"How black is it?" Michael demanded.

"It's far too early to say," Hennessy said at last; he mumbled rather. "I've often been on cases which have looked quite straightforward at first and have become so complicated you wouldn't believe. Last thing I would do is to take it for granted that Hester is guilty."

Guilty.

Winterton, still looking down his nose, gave what

seemed to be a sly, satisfied smile. "*I* take it for granted," he seemed to imply.

Then Hennessy said: "And after all, if she did kill him, it could have been in self-defence, it isn't necessarily murder. I shouldn't take anything for granted, Mike. Er—Ally, I only wish someone else had this job to do. Believe me, I'll help in every way I can."

Alicia didn't answer as Hennessy went out.

"I don't want him in my house again," she declared, when the door had closed.

"I know how you feel," Michael said.

"I mean it."

"Of course you do."

"Mike," Alicia said, and then caught her breath and felt tears stinging her eyes. "Mike, what's happened? Could Hester have——"

She broke off.

"Of course she didn't kill the man," Michael said. This was the first time he had raised his voice since he had talked to her about Hester. "It's unthinkable—good God, don't *you* start doubting her."

Alicia said: "I don't doubt her, Mike, don't say that. Oh, if only she would ring up, if only we could talk to her."

As she said that, she realised that in fact she did doubt Hester; it was almost as if she knew that Hester had been in the car with that man, that Hester had run away from him, after——

"I hope Mannering doesn't rebuff young Guy," Michael said, in better control of himself. "Guy didn't lose any time, anyhow."

Alicia said: "No."

She thought: "Guy must have heard some frightening things to make him brave the Hall, Lord Horton, the reputation of John Mannering, all the things which might be expected to overawe him. How long would it be before he came back? What kind of reception would he have from Mannering? Would he get past the footman who would open the great front door? Lord Horton, the Mannerings and people like them still lived in a different world. Why should they interest themselves in this world which had been so happy and was now filled with such fear?"

She thought: "It wouldn't be so bad if there was something we could do."

"Make a cup of tea, sweet, and when we've had it we can start telephoning all of Hester's friends, to find out if they knew what was worrying her," Michael said. "I know it's late, but we can't sit doing nothing."

That was the moment when Guy cycled out of the range of the headlamp beams bunched near the gates of the Hall, the lights shining on the beech and birch trees there, still thin with the leaves of spring. Here, the only light was that of his own lamp, the only noises was the hum of the dynamo and the whir of the tyres on the gravel. The trunks of trees loomed up; the fresh green of saplings, even the pink eyes of rabbits. It was heavy going. He had scorned a three-speed for years, but on an uphill run which was urgent wished that he had one. The drive was over a mile long, and uphill all the way. He had come along here once or twice before, to play cricket on the private ground, and knew just how it twisted and turned. He had never cycled up by night, and it was eerie, even a little unnerving, although he would never had admitted it, except perhaps to his father. Sharp sounds startled him, as if people were walking about the woods on either side, but he saw no movement except that of the rabbits. It was a clear night, but the stars were visible only through the gap between the tops of the trees, which almost interlaced fifty or sixty feet above his head.

Then he saw a greater expanse of the star-filled sky, and knew that he was out of the worst of the woods; two or three more bends would bring him within sight of the Hall itself. Over on the left, hidden by a ring of fine oaks, was the cricket ground and the tennis courts, and more recently the swimming-pool installed when the present Lord Horton had taken over, about three years ago. There had been a lot of talk about his unworthiness, but since he had taken residence little had been said against him, for he spent money freely in the village, he had taken on more men for the grounds, and paid good wages. It was part of the new policy at the Hall that some custom should be given to local tradesmen and farmers; hence the weekly order for the Vanes.

Guy was letting thoughts like these run through his mind. With them were anxious moments when he thought of what had been said about Hester; the certainty with which his policemen friends had said that she had been seen with the dead man only an hour or two before the body had been discovered. And mingled with them was a curious kind of excitement at the prospect of meeting John Mannering. He could not remember the time when Mannering had not been a kind of hero to him, mostly as a legendary figure often talked about in the newspapers. He was known to be daring, known to take great risks to help those in trouble, known to defy the police if he thought it necessary.

Now that he was approaching the Hall, Guy found doubts creeping in, implanted by his mother's reaction. All he had heard about Mannering might be a kind of newspaper build-up. True, he'd given a pleasant enough smile when he had nearly backed into Guy, and had called out an apology, but that signified nothing.

Lights shone out from the Hall.

From there, three hundred yards away, the great building seemed not only massive but dark and forbidding. It was a centuries-old castle, once nearly a ruin, but rebuilt only fifty or sixty years ago. It stretched, as if with ramparts, for nearly seventy yards, and was almost as deep. There were castellated towers and walls; archers' slits in the grey Portland stone; narrow windows built in mock-Norman style. The reconstruction was known to have cost the first Lord Horton—the multi-millionaire ship-owner—half a million pounds.

Yet the lights gave the blackness of the building a warmth and a kind of friendliness.

Guy felt small and insignificant as he cycled towards the porticoed doorway. He found himself wondering whether he should go to the back, or boldly to the front door. Anyone arriving at the front on a bicycle had a nerve. He began to grin, and as the ground levelled out, put on speed. Now he could see the shape of the lighted windows, tall and arched, on either side of the doorway; there were seven lights showing in all, one of them outside the great entrance porch. Guy drew up by this, and got off his machine. He hesitated before leaning it against one of the pillars; that was almost a sacrilege. He grinned, and said *sotto voce:* "They can't eat me." He went boldly to the front door, saw the great hanging bell-pull, searched for an ordinary bell-push and saw none. He held the iron handle and pulled sharply; there was a scratchy noise above his head but no sound of a ringing bell.

He drew back, listening intently.

He knew one or two of the servants at the Hall, and wasn't sure whether to hope that someone he knew opened the door or not; a man who didn't know that he was Guy Vane might give him a better hearing. The door opened quickly enough to startle him, and he was confronted by a small, dark-clad man whom he had seen about Gilston town, but whom he didn't know.

"Good evening, sir."

"Good evening," Guy said, and wished that his mouth didn't seem so dry. "Is Mr. Man—may I see Mr. Mannering, please?"

"I will find out if he is in," the small man said, and stood aside.

Guy stepped in.

He was dwarfed by the enormous hall, startled by the walls of stone furnished with great tapestries. The walls had iron rings in them, some filled with electric lights made in the shape of torches. More of these went up the walls of the great curved staircase which led to a gallery high above his head. This had been meant to impress; now it could easily overawe anyone new to it. Guy made an effort not to be overawed, but was acutely conscious of his grey flannels and tweed coat, his bicycle clips, the fact that he was sweating after the hard ride.

"What name shall I tell Mr. Mannering, sir?" The 'sir' did not seem to have any edge to it.

"Vane—Guy Vane."

"Thank you, sir." The small man turned away and walked towards a double doorway behind the circular staircase; the hall ran right round the staircase, with a few doors, all big and iron studded, leading off it. The double doors opened, and Guy was alone here. He looked round, craning his neck now that there was no need to maintain any kind of pretence. Everything was so vast that it was almost comical. He could imagine his father coming in, looking round, and making pertinent, ironic comments; it would take a great deal to overawe his father.

Then he was aware of being watched. A slight noise attracted his attention at first coming from the staircase. He looked up. It seemed an age before he picked out the figure of a young man standing by one of the great pillars which supported the gallery. He knew the man, slightly; had once played cricket and once played soccer against him. This was the Honourable Rodney Horton, the only son of Lord Horton, and heir to the Hall and everything that went with it. That more than anything else affected Guy: he was looking at a man not more than four or five years older than himself, but who would inherit several million pounds.

Young Horton did not look away from him, but raised a hand in a casual greeting. Then the small man came from the double doors behind the stairs.

"Mr. Mannering will see you, sir."

Guy only just checked himself from exclaiming: "Oh, good!" He was near the double doors when a clock he hadn't noticed because it was hidden by the staircase began to chime. It was midnight; what a time to burst in. If Mannering was willing to see him now, it was reasonable proof that he was everything that his reputation claimed.

The small man led the way into a room large by the bungalow standards, but small here. A log fire in an old open hearth smouldered. The walls were plastered and painted, and several portraits hung on them, but Guy was not interested in furniture or paintings, only in Mannering, who was standing with his back to the fire. He was alone. He looked tall and quite remarkably handsome, and what was more important, he looked as if he belonged here. By his side was a small table which was probably centuries old; on it stood a squat bottle of brandy and two big brandy glasses. The glow of the fire reflected on the glasses, and made the brandy in one of them look as if it were tinged with blood.

"Hallo!" Mannering greeted, as Guy found himself shaking hands; and also found himself attracted by the other's smile, and the glint in his eyes. "Didn't we try to run each other down earlier this evening?"

"That's right," Guy said. "I—er—it's extremely good of you to see me."

"I can't imagine it's a social call so late as this," Mannering said dryly. "If it's urgent enough to come so late, it must be important." He hesitated, as if giving Guy time to adjust himself, and then asked in the mildest of voices: "Is it about your sister?"

CHAPTER SIX

PROMISE

JOHN MANNERING thought: "I like the look of him."

He saw the startled expression in the youngster's grey eyes, and the eagerness, too. He liked the upright figure, and the squared shoulders, as well as a look of fearlessness and simplicity seldom found in a youth of eighteen or so.

"How on earth did you guess that it was about Hester?" Guy Vane demanded.

There was no point in mystifying him; no reason why he should not be told the obvious things, even though there was a great deal that no one but Mannering and his host yet knew.

"It's very simple," Mannering answered. "No witchcraft I assure you. As the murder was committed in the grounds of the Hall, Lord Horton telephoned the Chief Constable, who told him everything there is to know so far—that this murdered man was known to have been with a Miss Hester Vane this evening, and earlier in the day. So when Guy Vane calls——" he broke off with a shrug.

Guy said: "It sounds easy, when you explain it like that." His eyes narrowed and hardened, he could be quite a tough customer. "I don't believe that my sister killed this man. Do the police think she did?"

How much could he take?

Mannering said: "Yes, I'm pretty sure they do."

He saw the other's jaws clench, saw them work for a moment, saw the stubbornness in his expression. There was no real shock, just a realisation of unpleasant facts and a determination not to accept them.

"Well, they're wrong."

"Sure?" asked Mannering.

"Of course I'm——" Guy began, but hesitated. When Mannering did not prompt him, he went on carefully: "In a way I'm sure, because I'm positive that whatever happened, Hester wouldn't kill a man. On the other hand, I can't offer any evidence, if that's what you mean."

"Good distinction." Mannering said, and wondered if he were a little too ponderous. "Did you know the dead man?"

"I've seen him, but I didn't know him."

"Do you know what connection there was between him and your sister?"

"Mr. Mannering, all I can tell you is that I don't believe that Hester would do anything which was—well, criminal. She was a bit troubled about something, but none of us knows what it was. My mother's worried stiff, and my father—well, there was a policeman at the house just before I left, and I heard what the police were saying among themselves. To hear them talk it was just a question of finding my sister and accusing her. I don't believe it, but I can't *do* much. Will you help?"

It was very straight from the shoulder; like the boy.

"Are you sure you know what you're asking?" Mannering asked.

"I think so, sir."

"I mean, what happens if I try to help and find that the evidence points to your sister?"

"I don't believe it will."

"It might."

Guy hesitated, and then said roughly: "Well, if she did it, she did it, and there's nothing we can do except try to find out why. If the man attacked her, or anything like that, wouldn't it be justifiable homicide?"

"Yes," Mannering agreed, and wondered how much anxiety the boy could really stand. He did not speak too seriously, but did not want to appear too casual.

"But there's no evidence of a struggle, no evidence that the dead man expected to be killed. He was sitting at the wheel of his car. There wasn't room for him to have made any sudden movement towards a passenger, the wheel would have prevented him. It looks as if he was sitting there, probably talking, when he was killed with a knife wound from the side—the passenger's side. It pierced the carotid artery."

He saw the boy flinch; so obviously he knew the implications of that injury.

Mannering went on, feeling cold-blooded and cruel but knowing that all of this had to be said:

"It could have been done quite easily by anyone, man or woman, sitting next to Morgan——"

"Who?"

"The dead man's name was Clive Morgan."

"Oh."

"Ever heard your sister talk of 'Clive'?"

"No."

That seemed the truth.

"I see. Well, it's almost certain a passenger inflicted the wound. If there had been any sign of a struggle, if the body had been found in the back of the car where there was comfortable room for movement, or even by the side of the car, it might lend colour to the theory that whoever killed him was defending himself or herself, but there's no evidence of this. The indications are that Morgan was sitting and talking, and was killed by a single thrust. A knife thrust to the neck isn't made without intent to kill," Mannering added dryly.

"I can see that," Guy said. "Have you actually seen the body?"

"I saw Morgan while he was in the car."

"Do the—do the newspapers know about this?"

"Two local reporters were there."

"Well, my mother will have to be told before she reads it in the newspapers," Guy said. He drew his hand across his forehead, and Mannering belatedly offered cigarettes. "No, thanks," Guy replied. "I don't smoke yet." The 'yet' seemed to emphasise his youth. "I—er—I wouldn't mind a glass of cider or lemonade, or——"

"I'll get it," Mannering said at once, and went to a Cromwellian court cupboard, where drinks were kept. He was aware of the intentions of the lad watching him, and wondered what was coming next and how far he dare go on. How much did it matter, for instance, if young Vane was told the truth about Clive Morgan, and talked about it in the village or in the town? The newspapers might have the story already, so the truth was that it would make very little difference. Mannering poured out cider, took the tankard to the boy and said: "Did your mother suspect that your sister was being blackmailed?"

Guy exclaimed: "*What!*" and started so violently that a little of the cider spilled over the edge of the tankard. His eyes looked enormous. "Are you sure?"

"It's a reasonable assumption. Morgan is believed to have been a blackmailer. He was known to be a rogue."

"Good God!"

"And if you're going to say that he deserved to be killed, I wouldn't argue," Mannering remarked, dryly. "But the police take the view that the victim of a blackmailer should tell them, not take the law into their own hands. Do you know if your sister was short of money?"

Guy didn't answer.

"Did you?" Mannering asked, more firmly.

"Yes," Guy answered, slowly and reluctantly. "Yes, I did. She wanted to borrow twenty-five pounds from me about a month ago. I'd only got about a fiver. Could have done with it back last week, so I dropped a hint, but she didn't take it. I guessed that she was still hard up. I couldn't really understand it, because she gets a good salary—and——" Guy broke off and narrowed his eyes. "Do you think that this man was blackmailing *her*?"

"I've told you that it looks like it," Mannering said. "She was seen talking to him about once a week, usually on the road from your home to Gilston—as if he met her there by appointment. It was always on a Friday—she gets paid on Thursday, doesn't she?"

"Yes."

"She had borrowed from friends at her work, too, and drawn an advance on her salary," Mannering went on. "The police haven't had much time to work in, but they'd started an inquiry before Morgan was killed, because he wasn't trusted. They suspected that he was up to no good with your sister, and checked—that's how they came to find out that she owed altogether about a hundred and fifty pounds."

"A hundred and——" Guy's voice trailed off.

"That's a lot of money," Mannering said flatly.

"It's a hell of a lot," Guy agreed weakly, and pressed his hand against his forehead. "I hardly know whether to be glad or sorry that I came to see you, sir. This is shocking. *Awful.* But—but if he did drive her too far, wouldn't that be justifiable homicide? I mean, would it be considered provocation?" He was almost pathetically eager.

"That would probably depend on what she'd done to allow him to blackmail her," Mannering replied, cautiously, "and how long it had been going on. Do you know what she'd done?"

Guy didn't answer.

Mannering saw him sip the cider, which he had hardly touched, then saw him turn and put the tankard down, as if he had no more patience. He still did not speak, and his face was something to see; tense, handsome, young-old. He was fighting a kind of personal battle, and it would be a mistake to interrupt until it was over. The room was quiet, there was not even a rustle of hot ash on the hearth; but suddenly a clock struck; it was twelve o'clock.

Guy said: "No, sir, and that's the strangest thing

about it. I can't believe that Hester would do anything which would let a blackmailer get his claws into her, unless—well, unless she was having an affair with someone, and it had gone too far. She would know that my mother and father would hate that, and—but it doesn't make any sense," he exploded, his eyes blazing. "No, I don't know. I just can't believe that Hester would commit any crime to explain blackmail. It must be something else."

"And you want me to find out?"

"I'd give anything if you would." Guy spread his hands, not knowing that he had copied the gesture from his father. "That's easy to say, I haven't really got anything to offer, but I'd do anything to repay you. It isn't only Hester, it——"

He broke off.

Mannering didn't prompt him.

"I was going to say it's my mother and father," Guy went on, "and then I realised that we don't know where Hester is. If—if she did do this thing, she mightn't have the—the courage to face up to it." He was losing colour, and the brightness in his eyes seemed to be almost feverish. "If—if she struck at him and killed him, she might have——"

He could not bring himself to finish.

Mannering said: "Take it easy, Guy. There's no reason at all to think she might have killed herself."

Guy said tensely: "I heard them arranging a search of the copse, and of the woods on the estate. I thought they were looking for clues, but if the police think that she might have killed herself, they would start a search at night, wouldn't they? They'd be more likely to leave clues until the morning."

"They might," Mannering agreed.

"Oh, God!" Guy exclaimed. "It's going to be terrible if——" he stopped again, and squared his shoulders, gave Mannering a young-old look, and spoke much more carefully, pausing between every few words. "I don't know what's got into me, sir. I seem to be assuming that Hester killed this man. I don't believe she did. She must be hiding somewhere, terribly frightened. Will you help to find her, and will you look after her interests, Mr. Mannering?"

Mannering answered promptly: "Yes."

The boy raised his hands, as if he had expected a refusal and could not fully comprehend such swift acceptance. He hesitated for what seemed a long time, before saying:

"I can't thank you enough, Mr. Mannering. I mean that. I—I would like to go and tell my mother and father. Will you come and see them in the morning?"

"I'll come and see them now," Mannering said, 'and run you home. Did you come on your bike?"

"Yes."

"We'll dump that in the boot," Mannering said, talking as unceremoniously about his Rolls-Bentley as Guy would about the market garden van. "Let's go round to the garage." He moved briskly to the door and Guy followed almost to quickly; they got in each other's way. Mannering stood back. The boy was nearly six feet; he was going to be powerful when he filled out. He moved very well, too, and was so obsessed by the disaster which had overtaken his sister and the family that he hardly spared a moment to glance about him. It took them several minutes to reach a side door of the Hall, another minute to reach the garages, hidden by a front wing, and still lit up. The Rolls-Bentley was drawn a little ahead of a Rolls-Royce, a Daimler, a Chrysler, a Jaguar and an M.G. A man in blue chauffeur's uniform came hurrying as they put the bicycle into the boot of Mannering's car.

"All right, Symes, I'll drive," Mannering said. "In you get, Guy."

Guy climbed in, sat in the unbelievable luxury, and realised it without feeling the slightest excitement. He sensed the expertness with which Mannering took the controls, and the smoothness of the car as they started down the drive. The great headlights carved a silver light through the night, then fell upon the trees and silvered the pale green of young leaves. Still purring, the car nosed its way downhill and round the sharp bends. The beams of the headlamps seemed to dart among the trees and the undergrowth, disturbing rabbits and a hare, suddenly lighting up the green eyes of a fox, which slunk across the road. Then they turned another bend. In that instant, the night was filled with dozens of lamps. There were car headlamps, cycle lamps, storm lanterns and torches, the smaller lights on the move, obviously being carried by the police as they searched.

Guy said gruffly: "Well, we know what they think now, sir, don't we?"

"The police can get things wrong," Mannering answered, and did not add the thing which was uppermost in his mind. It was wholly irrational, but it had been there from the moment he had seen this lad.

If his sister was anything like him, she might commit murder if driven to it, but she would not kill herself.

If she had not killed herself, had she run away from fear of the consequences, or had she been taken away against her will?

That idea wasn't yet in the boy's mind; probably was not in the mind of anyone but his.

Mannering slowed down, because two men were crossing the drive; as he did so, he heard the shrill blast of a policeman's whistle. He glanced sharply at Guy Vane, and saw from the boy's expression that he had jumped to the obvious conclusion: that the blowing of the whistle might mean that the police had found Hester.

CHAPTER SEVEN

THE EVIDENCE

MANNERING pulled into the side of the drive, and let the nearest nearside front wheel rise on to the bank as he stopped. Dozens of men were hurrying towards the spot where one had blown his whistle. The copse was thin just here, and there were few small trees, so that it was possible to see three men, standing together and staring down at a particular spot. Mannering heard Guy Vane mutter under his breath, and did not stop him from flinging open the door of the car and jumping on to the drive. Guy did not notice that Mannering actually got out of his door more quickly, and was a little ahead of him as he made for the small group.

Then Detective Inspector Hennessy and Detective Sergeant Winterton, whom Mannering had met earlier in the evening, pushed their way through towards the centre. Guy began to run; but there was no need, for nobody lay on the ground; instead, there was something quite small. As he drew nearer, Mannering saw that it was like a piece of rag; nearer still, it proved to be a scarf which looked blue in the bright light of a man's torch.

Hennessy and the sergeant bent down to examine it, but no one touched it.

Guy stopped short.

Mannering touched his arm, and he glanced round.

"Keep your voice low," Mannering said. "Do you recognise it?"

"I think so."

"What is it?"

"My—my sister's scarf."

"Right," Mannering said. "Wait here. If the police

ask you to go forward you'd better go, but don't volunteer to do or say anything. I won't be long." He went ahead, and two or three men who looked as if they would like to stop him, glanced up, recognised him, and stepped hastily out of the way. He reached the local detectives as they bent down, Winterton actually crouching over the knitted scarf. A man with a camera was coming forward.

Hennessy saw Mannering, and snapped: "Stop there."

Mannering stopped, and asked mildly: "What's the point of stopping?"

"Sorry, Mr. Mannering." Hennessy was stiff-voiced. "I don't want anyone on this spot until the ground's been thoroughly examined. Sergeant Carter!" A man came hurrying. "I want a protecting fence put up round this spot, quick, and a guard every twenty yards or so. No one's to come through. Willis, take photographs from all angles, but be careful where you tread. Mind that." He pointed, and Mannering saw a patch of soft ground with some footprints in it but he couldn't be sure whether they were a woman's or a man's. "Anything I can do for you, sir?" Hennessy now asked.

"Any sign of the missing girl?"

"This scarf answers the description of one that she was known to have been wearing today."

"Any sign of anyone else near here?"

Hennessy was very formal as he had been all the time; apparently he did not relish carrying out his investigation in the grounds of the Hall, nor relish having to give orders to a friend of Lord Horton.

"Sorry, sir, I've no comment to make."

Mannering said: "Pity," and turned and went back to Guy, who had obeyed instructions, and hadn't moved. He had been within earshot, and was staring at the scarf. At a touch from Mannering, he turned and went back to the Rolls-Bentley. He did not speak until they were on the move again.

"It looked like hers."

"I think we can be sure she was here," said Mannering. "How far is this from the car?"

"About two hundred yards, I suppose."

"A long way off for her to drop her scarf," observed Mannering, but the boy did not take inference from that, and Mannering did not make the implication any more obvious. They neared the open drive gates. Only a few police stood about now, and two or three local people were still excited enough to watch them. As Mannering turned right, towards Gilston and the Vanes' home, the headlights of a car behind shone on to his driving-mirror, and once on the road, he slowed down. The other car passed. Mannering saw the driver wave him down, and pulled into the side of the road. The other car, the Jaguar, pulled in front of him, and the driver jumped out and came hurrying back.

"That's Lord Horton," Guy said, sharply.

"Yes," Mannering agreed, winding down his window. He saw Horton's heavy, rather fleshy face, clear in the reflected light of the headlamps. "Hallo, Barry," he greeted. "What's brought you?"

Horton looked past him, at the boy.

"Good evening, Vane. John, I want a word with you, urgently."

"Right," said Mannering. "It won't take long, will it?"

"Two minutes."

"I'll get out," Guy offered swiftly, and before Mannering could attempt to stop him, he was out of the Rolls-Bentley and standing in the road looking back at the flickering and the swaying lights to the spot where the murdered man had been found. Mannering also got out. Horton was breathing heavily, as if he had been hurrying before getting into the car. He was half a head shorter than Mannering, but probably eight inches further round the waist; a certain forty-four.

"Where are you going, John?"

"To have a word with the Vanes."

"You know this boy is her brother, don't you?"

"I don't believe that much is coincidence," Mannering said. "I like the boy."

"I liked the girl. It looks as if she's a murderer."

"You ought to be glad about that."

"John," said Horton, in a very quiet voice, and gripping Mannering's arm, "you know the position as well if not better than anyone else. No one wanted Morgan dead more than I, no one is more glad that he's dead. You also know that I couldn't have killed him, because you were sitting in my room with me when he died. I'm sorry that the girl's involved, especially as Rod is fond of her, but the vital thing is to make sure that no one realised that my son was being blackmailed."

"If Rod gets scared over this, he might tell you more about who was blackmailing him."

"You know it was Morgan."

"I know Morgan was someone's catspaw," Mannering said.

"Rod doesn't know whose. It's vital that no one discovers that Morgan was blackmailing him, I tell you. If the police were to probe and find that out, and why, it would be disastrous for the family name."

"It would be disastrous for that girl if she were convicted for a murder she didn't commit."

"She must have committed it!"

"That's what the police seem to think, that's what you want to think, and that's what we have to prove. Barry, I'll go a long way to help you, and you know it. I've done a lot already and——"

"Don't think that I'm not grateful," Horton said, in a louder voice. He took Mannering's forearm and drew closer, so that he could speak without any risk of being overheard by Guy or anyone else nearby. In fact Guy was on the other side of the car from them, and out of sight; but that did not mean that he could not hear. "I'm so grateful that I'll do anything you ask," Horton went on. "You've been magnificent. But you mustn't spoil it now. There's no need for you to get any more deeply involved. The police don't like the idea of you taking part in the investigation. I told you that the Chief Constable said so. There's no need for you to do a thing except stay here and check these things of mine, and make sure just what is missing."

"And what if the girl's convicted?"

"John, you don't even know her."

"If she's alive, I'm going to," Mannering said. His voice was pleasant, and his expression matched it; but there was something in the way he spoke which made it obvious that nothing would change his mind. "I won't give anything away about Rod," he went on, "but the police are probably already asking themselves why you came chasing after me when I was taking young Vane home. You not only have to be careful, you have to make sure that Rod stops playing the fool, too."

"I can't answer for Rodney," Horton said, and there was a note almost of bitterness in his voice. "You're the one who can see me through. And for the sake of a girl you've never even seen."

"I saw her this afternoon," Mannering said. "You said that she usually went to tea at Madden's. She was there with her mother. I had a good look at them both when they left—after a tiff, I think." Mannering rested a hand firmly on Horton's shoulder. "Barry, there's no reason at all why this should make more trouble for you."

"I hope you're right, but I don't like it."

"Forget it," Mannering advised. He turned away and raised his voice: "Guy!" he called. "We're ready to start."

There was no answer.

"Vane!" he called.

There was still no answer.

He moved swiftly round the front of the Rolls-Bentley, and stared along the road on the far side.

THE EVIDENCE

There was no sign of Vane. He peered into the trees on either side but the only light was from the two cars and no beam was shining into the trees. He felt a surge of annoyance with himself for having let this happen and turned to face Horton, who was standing very still, big, and burly, only the darkness hiding his obesity. It also hid his expression.

"He's gone off in a huff. The less you have to do with that family the better," Horton said. "Come back and forget him."

"I'll be back later," Mannering said, brusquely. "Good night."

He got back into the car.

He was not often completely nonplussed, as he was now. If anything had seemed certain, it was that young Vane would stand by the side of the car. Had he heard the beginning of the conversation and jumped to conclusions which made him turn against him, Mannering? Or had he grown tired of waiting, and decided to walk on? His home was at least three miles away and his bicycle was still in the boot of the big car. If he had decided to walk, he was probably expecting to be picked up at any moment.

Horton was standing and watching Mannering.

"Give it up, John," he urged.

Mannering thought: "I hope I haven't let you fool me, Barry," waved and started off. The car hardly made a sound as it rolled forward along the wide road. Not far ahead the wooded land became thinner, and soon there were meadows on either side, open to the sky. Mannering did not see the shape of a man nor hear the sound of anyone walking. He judged that he had driven half a mile, and doubted whether there had been time for young Vane to have walked so far, but drove on another half mile. Then he was quite sure that no one could have walked the distance in that time. He watched for a side turning, and reversed into it. He was feeling real alarm now.

He reached the spot where he and Horton had talked, recognising a signpost near it. The Jaguar had gone. He stopped the engine and peered ahead into the darkness; they were half a mile from the scene of the murder and from the bustling activity of the police. Would Guy Vane have gone back to talk to Hennessy?

It was the last thing Mannering would have expected.

His hand was on the ignition key again, to start the engine, and he was trying to make up his mind what to do when he heard a sound which startled him. He waited, tensely, listening for a repetition; and suddenly it came.

Someone was calling, and now the word was clear on the still night air.

"Help!" a man cried. "Help!"

CHAPTER EIGHT

DANGER LIST

MANNERING moved on the instant that he recognised the single word. He snatched a flashlight from the pocket of the door nearest him, thrust the door open, and jumped out. The cry came again, and seemed a little more clear.

"*Help!*"

Mannering pressed the horn of the car and it blared out S O S. He kept it up just long enough to repeat the signal, then ran towards the woods and the direction of the cry.

He heard the cry again, and could only guess where it came from, but his torch shone on the thick trunks of trees and on dense undergrowth. He had to twist this way and that, it was almost impossible to keep his bearings.

"*Help!*" the cry came.

He raised his voice: "*Where are you?*"

"*Help!*"

"*That's—right. Keep—shouting.*"

Thoughts flashed through Mannering's mind. That this was Guy Vane; that if he had been attacked, as Morgan had, he must have escaped or he could not keep calling; that the desperation in his cry told of terrifying urgency, which probably meant that others were near, and menacing him; if they were, they would be waiting for Mannering, able to hear him as he forced his way towards the spot.

"*Help!*"

It was much nearer, and undoubtedly came from the right. Mannering turned towards it.

"*What's wrong?*"

"*Two men—look out!*"

"*Just keep shouting.*"

As Mannering's voice faded, silence fell. The interval between Guy's calls seemed to get longer. Then, they stopped. Why? Mannering found himself longing for a call. Here in darkness broken only by the single beam of light, danger could strike from the right, from the left or from behind him.

"*Keep shouting!*"

There was no response.

Why had the youth stopped so abruptly? There had been no choked cry, no sudden scream of alarm; just the continuing quiet. The mystery of that made the situation worse, while Mannering became aware of shadows, as of men, creeping about the woods. They were not of men but the shapes of bushes and trees distorted by the beam of the torch, movements made by him alone.

He stopped in a small clearing, surrounded by the trees, and there was silence.

"Guy!" he called. "Where are you?"

Not far from this spot a man had died, killed by a knife wound, swift and silent. Had it happened again? How else had it been possible for anyone to silence the boy so swiftly and so completely.

"*Guy!*"

It was useless to shout any more, and it might make the danger greater; he might be attacked next, to give the boy's assailants time to get away. Mannering was acutely aware of this danger, and he went more slowly to the spot where he believed he had heard the last sound. He might be wasting his time, might be going round in circles, but he could not give up yet.

Then he heard a moan.

He stopped, and swung the beam towards the sound. It came again. He swung the torch round, lighting up the saplings, a thicket, hawthorn, and the fat trunks of oak trees. He saw a huddled figure on the ground beneath one of the trees, and heard a moan. He jumped forward, and doing so, caught sight of a man moving stealthily on his right.

He pretended not to notice, but hurried to the huddled figure. Dark, glossy hair was towards him, and he was sure that this was Guy. He darted a glance towards the left and saw that the man was drawing nearer, keeping a little way behind. Mannering glanced in the other direction, but saw no one else. Staring down at Guy, he went down on one knee, then shifted his position so that the trunk of a tree protected him at the back; he could not be taken by surprise from there.

The boy's face looked starkly pale in the bright torchlight. His black eyebrows showed up vividly. His eyes were closed and his mouth was slack. There was no sign of blood at his throat, nothing to suggest that he had been wounded with a knife. Watching from beneath his lashes, tensed up because he was sure that he was going to be attacked, Mannering felt the boy's long, strong limbs; none seemed broken. Then he saw the ugly wound at the base of the neck.

Guy had almost certainly fainted from loss of blood, or from exhaustion.

Mannering glanced up. There was an overhanging branch of an oak tree; Guy must have been perched on that, wounded and calling for help, and then collapsed and fallen. Not only Mannering but his assailant had been looking for him. Had the assailant been planning to finish him off?

The man had edged round so that he could approach from Mannering's left. Mannering began to talk to the boy in undertones, to create the impression that he could think of nothing else. He heard the rustle of movement, the faint crack of a twig trodden into the ground. The man stopped, as if fearful of being heard, then came on again. He was nearly within striking distance, and he had a weapon in his hand, like an old knopkeirie, but with a spiked ball-shaped head. Such a weapon could have inflicted the wound on Guy's neck.

Any moment, the man would leap and strike.

Mannering tensed himself, only one thought in his mind: to get a prisoner. A moment's misjudgement would be fatal.

The man leapt.

Mannering swivelled round, still crouching, flung himself at the other's ankles, clutched and pulled. He felt the man topple, heard him gasp. He jumped to his feet as the other fell backwards, the weapon falling from his fingers, and Mannering felt a moment of exultation, because it had worked so perfectly. Before the victim had a chance to recover he could be knocked out; then it would be a simple matter of fetching help.

That was when he saw the movement from his right, and realised that there was a second man. He had to turn away from the one who had fallen. He saw the other, short and stocky, strangely distorted in the reflected light from the torch. He met a full-blooded assault with both fists, but the weight of the other man's attack carried him back. He caught the torch with his heel, and it went out.

There was pitch darkness.

He felt the heavy, stocky body brush against him, struck out, and landed a blow which brought a grunt of pain.

A man muttered: "Come on."

"We've got to get——"

"Let's get out of here!"

The darkness made it very eerie. Any moment a beam of light might shine out, but there would be great danger for the others if they used a torch; the light would tell him where they were. He heard their heavy breathing, their whispering. One wanted to go, the other to stay and finish the job. Close by Mannering lay Guy Vane, unconscious, and Mannering could not leave this spot without Guy.

Then, a long way off, he heard a whistle; a police

whistle. He raised his voice and shouted, the only one useful word.

"*Help!*"

That would carry for hundreds of yards.

A man muttered: "Shut him up."

"*Help!*"

"Shut him——" the speaker began. Then came a louder rustling among the trees, and Mannering stood still and tense, knowing that he might be viciously attacked, that the others might be able to pick out his figure against the light-coloured trunk of the tree. The rustling seemed to become louder. He backed against a tree. The whistle sounded again, and was nearer.

"*Come on!*" one of the men gasped.

Mannering heard the rustling getting further and further away. Then a beam of light shot out, at least twenty yards off. Against it he saw the figures of the two men, one so short and stocky, the other taller and leaner, as they hurried away.

Not far off in the other direction came the cry: "*Where are you?*"

Now there were powerful lights coming towards Mannering as he knelt over the boy, who lay as still as death. Mannering's torchlight attracted the police, who came crashing through the undergrowth, going all round him because they were not sure who he was. Then one of the men recognised him, and another called:

"How's that boy?"

"It's touch and go," Mannering said, and knew that it was true.

Alicia Vane said for the third time in five minutes: "It's after one o'clock." In fact it was nearly half-past one. No one had called and there had been no message since the police had left and the call had come from Guy. It was nearly an hour and a half since they had finished telephoning, and the result had been negligible; they knew nothing more about Hester, and Guy hadn't come home.

"You must ring the Hall again," Alicia said, swinging round on Michael. "We just can't sit here. Either we must ring the Hall or ring the police."

"Ally, Lord Horton himself spoke to me, and promised to telephone the minute Mannering got back."

"He probably forgot all about it the moment he put down the receiver."

"He said he would leave a message in Mannering's room," Michael said. "We can't make nuisances of ourselves."

Something seemed to snap in Alicia's mind. She had been trying to keep calm, fighting against the desire to shout and cry, but now she gave up the struggle. One part of her mind knew that she was wrong, the other part accepted the inevitability of raging at Michael. She stood close to him, knowing that her eyes were glittering and her cheeks very pale, spitting words at him.

"What's happened to you? Have you lost your mind? How can you stand there and talk about making nuisances of ourselves when our children might be in deadly danger? I always knew you were spineless, I didn't think you were this much of a coward. Stand away from that telephone. *I'll* talk to his precious lordship, even if it means getting him out of bed."

"Ally," Michael said, in a very quiet voice, "it won't help."

"It's got to help. Even if we make a *nuisance* of ourselves to his lordship, even if we make a *nuisance* of ourselves to Mr. John Mannering, even if we make a *nuisance* of ourselves to the police, we have to do something to help our children."

"Ally, Guy will be all right."

"You don't know that he will be all right, and I'm

not going to be smarmed over. For all you know he might be in as much danger as Hester. And who is this man Mannering? He might be a criminal himself. Just because he gets his name in the newspaper and because the noble lord makes a fuss of him, there's no guarantee of his integrity. And Guy's in trouble. He wouldn't have kept away so late if he weren't—he would have sent a message. You know he would. Hester would have sent a message if she'd been able to. I did nothing about that, but I don't intend to stand aside and do nothing about this, and if you haven't the courage to do it, I will."

She knew how much she was hurting, and almost hated herself for some of the things she was saying; but she could not stop herself. Fear drove her into more and more abuse and reproach. She had a presentiment that all was not well with Guy, that when news came it would be bad.

"Please stand away from the telephone," she requested, coldly.

"All right, Ally," Michael said. The quietness of his voice and the gentleness of his manner made a reproach in themselves. He stood aside. Alicia touched the telephone and looked into the street beyond the front garden, seeing the darkness, for the street lamps were put out at midnight. Then she saw a glow of light, as of a car coming some distance off. She did not lift the telephone but waited, mingled hope and dread rising in her.

It might be someone bringing Guy home.

It was too great a light for his bicycle.

If it passed she would lift the receiver and telephone the Hall. Then——

"It's slowing down!" Michael exclaimed. He turned and strode towards the door and the passage, and was opening the door before Alicia reached the passage itself. The car had stopped outside. Alicia saw a man get out, but did not recognise him. She waited to make sure that no one else followed him; that Guy was not there. Suddenly, awfully, hope was replaced by dread. She went rushing towards the front door as Michael opened it. The light fell on the face of John Mannering, still with that striking handsomeness which she had seen in the restaurant, but there was one difference.

He was not smiling.

Alicia could not make herself go forward, could only stand and stare at the visitor as Michael demanded:

"Have you seen our son?"

Before he answered, Mannering looked at Alicia, and she sensed that there was great compassion in him; the reason for it struck like a knife into her breast.

CHAPTER NINE

MANNERING

MANNERING sensed the turmoil in the minds of these two people as soon as he saw them. There was the man, so like his injured son, and the mother standing by a door, hands clenched and raised in front of her, eyes glittering, face very pale, as if she knew that he had brought bad news. For him, the worst of it was that he did not know for certain how bad it was.

He could have left this to the police, and for a moment half wished that he had. There were only seconds to wait before telling them, and the right words were difficult to find.

The right words were the simple words of truth.

"Yes," he said. "I've just come from the hospital. He's been injured, but he's in the best possible hands."

Michael Vane held the side of the door more tightly, and closed his eyes; that was the only sign he gave of the shock. Mrs. Vane dropped her hands. For a moment her body sagged, and Mannering thought that she would collapse. He actually moved forward, and his alarm must have shown in his face, for Vane swung round and reached his wife in a few long strides. She didn't fall, but leaned against him.

"How badly is he hurt?" he asked.

"Seriously," Mannering answered.

The woman as well as the man were looking at him, and there was bitter reproach in the woman's eyes; he could sense that she blamed him, and that mattered because he also blamed himself.

"Is he dead?" Vane steeled himself to ask.

"No, Mr. Vane."

"How seriously is he injured?"

"He's in the operating theatre at the Gilston Hospital now, and the medical opinion is that he has a very good chance."

Mrs. Vane echoed in a strange voice:

"*Chance?*"

"Alicia, come and sit down," her husband said.

"Chance," she repeated, and looked at Mannering as if she hated him. "What did you do to him? He came to see you, he trusted you, he believed in you. What did you do to my son?"

"Ally——"

"*Let him answer for himself!*"

Mannering thought: "It's worse than I feared" and told himself that it was partly due to the fact that this was the night's second shock. First the missing daughter and the suspicion of murder, now this: the man was holding up remarkably well, and once the woman had worked off her hysteria, she would, too; he must spark that hysteria, and draw it out.

"What did you do to my son?" She shook herself free of her husband's grasp, and strode towards Mannering. The door was still open. He stepped forward, pushing the door behind him, and answered much more sharply than he felt:

"I don't like your tone, Mrs. Vane."

She drew a deep breath, and stood still.

"Your son came to see me, unasked," he went on.

"I——"

"Why don't you tell us what you did to him? Why didn't you look after him? He's only a boy, couldn't you see that? He's only a boy. It's your fault that he's hurt."

"Is it my fault that your daughter is being hunted for murder?" Mannering asked, coldly. Something had to bring an eruption, and it had to come quickly.

"You devil!" Alicia Vane said in a taut voice. "How dare you come and call my daughter a murderess? Why, I could——"

She sprang forward, hand raised.

"Alicia!" Vane cried, and leapt after her.

She slapped Mannering in the face with such force that he staggered to one side. If her husband had not restrained her she would have slapped again and again, but after a moment or two a different expression appeared in her eyes, one of hopelessness rather than hysterical rage; as if she knew what she had done and the folly of it, but that did not matter.

"Both of them," she said helplessly. "Both of them."

"Do you know where my daughter is?" Vane demanded.

"No," answered Mannering.

"Are the police searching for her?"

"Yes."

"I see," said Vane, putting his arm round his wife's shoulders. "What happened to our son?"

Mannering told them, with great lucidity; then he told them about the finding of Hester's scarf in the woods, drew a vivid picture of the police search and the speed with which the police had come to Guy's assistance, and the urgency with which they had taken him to hospital. His voice warmed as he spoke, and the atmosphere eased. Vane was obviously trying to be rational, and his wife was emotionally exhausted but fighting to compose herself.

" . . . I made sure that there was nothing else that I could do, and came to see you," Mannering finished. "I thought you would prefer to hear from me than from the police."

"You're right about that," Vane said. "Thank you."

His wife made no comment, but looked intently at Mannering, as if seeing him more clearly. The reproach had vanished; she gave the impression that there was something about him which puzzled her.

"Because I don't think I agree with the police," Mannering went on.

Mrs. Vane's eyes sparkled.

"About my daughter?"

"Yes."

"The police think that she killed this man," Vane said, with a firmer note in his voice. "Don't you?"

"No."

"Have you any reason for saying that?"

Mannering had been here when these two had touched the depths of despair; it was strange to see the dawning of hope. For a long time they would be pulled both ways, but if he could make sure that they had real cause to hope, he would be able to save them from touching those depths again.

"Have you?" Mrs. Vane asked, sharply.

"I think so."

"What reason?"

"I think that Clive Morgan had made a lot of enemies, and more than one of them would have gladly murdered him," Mannering answered. "At least one of them was in the district tonight."

"Are you positive?"

"Yes."

"Do the police know?" Vane demanded.

"They know there were two men, but can't be sure that they murdered Morgan.' Mannering brushed a hand over his forehead, and added unexpectedly: "If there's one thing I'd like it's a cup of coffee. Could you possibly——"

"Of course," Mrs. Vane said, more naturally than she had spoken since he had arrived. "Don't say anything while I'm in the kitchen, though, I want to hear every word."

"Let's all go into the kitchen," Mannering suggested.

He watched the way Mrs. Vane bustled; kettle on, cups and saucers on a tray, biscuits out of a tin, everything hurried and yet orderly. Yet these were little indications that Mrs. Vane wasn't in control of herself. A chair by the wall of a narrow passage had footmarks on it, for instance, and some pieces of grass.

" . . . the first thing is to find Hester," Mannering said, flatly. "While the police are searching for her as a suspect they'll put in that little extra effort that would be lacking if they thought they had the murderer." That wasn't strictly true; but it would carry some weight, and was much better than saying that he wanted to keep some facts to himself, and that if he told the police that Clive Morgan had been blackmailing Rodney, the police would stop him working as he wanted to work; and as he thought was most effective.

Vane demurred:

"I'm not sure about that, Mannering."

"I think Mr. Mannering probably knows best," Mrs. Vane said, quite oblivious of the way she swung round to Mannering's side. "Mr. Mannering, you will do everything you can to help Hester, won't you?"

"Everything."

"Would you mind telling me why?" Vane asked.

"Mike, there's no need——"

"Because your son asked me to, because he ran into trouble while he was with me, and because I feel responsible for it," Mannering said. "And finally—my wife will tell you that I could never keep away from a murder investigation, I'll do everything I can simply because I want to find out the truth ahead of the police."

The kettle began to boil.

"Thank God you're here!" Mrs. Vane said. "Mike, will you go and get the van out, as soon as we've swallowed this cup of coffee we must get along to the hospital."

"Let me run you there," Mannering offered.

"We'll be better off with our own transport," Vane said. "Thanks all the same. I won't be two jiffs." He went out with a brisk step, and Mrs. Vane was still alert and comparatively cheerful. Mannering did not thrust his offer at them, but had coffee and biscuits and, just after half-past two, left the bungalow. Vane was already climbing up to the wheel of the van.

"Mike," Alicia said.

"We'll be there in ten minutes, and if the news were any worse we would have heard by now."

"I wasn't thinking of that," Alicia said, her voice very low-pitched. "There's a man in the garden."

"Don't be silly."

"I saw him when the headlights of Mr. Mannering's car shone along the shed."

"You're dreaming."

"Oh, don't be soft," Alicia said testily. "We ought to see who it is."

There was a long pause, and then Michael said: "I know who it is, Ally."

"What do you mean?"

"Didn't you expect the police to watch?"

"*Police?*"

"They're bound to be at the front as well as the back, in case——"

"Oh, of course," Alicia said. "What a fool I am. In case Hester comes home, you mean?"

"Yes."

"Mike!"

"What is it?"

"One of us ought to stay home."

"Why?"

"If she should come back or ring up, and find the house empty, it would be terrible."

"Oh," said Michael, in a tone which told her that he had not thought of that. There was a long pause, and then he went on: "Yes, you're right. I'd better stay here. Do you think Mrs. Parker would go into town with you?"

"I don't intend to ask her," Alicia said. "I'll drive myself; you can get a taxi in the morning. It's all right, Mike, I feel ten times better than I did. I don't know how he did it, but Mannering made me believe that everything will work out all right. I'll drive in, and I'll telephone you if there's any change in Guy's condition."

"All right," Michael conceded reluctantly. He did not say so, but it was almost too much to hope that Hester would get in touch with them. Alicia did not feel over-tired now, although at one time her head had ached so badly and her eyes had been so heavy that she had hardly known how to drag herself about the bungalow. Now she had to drive fast, to see Guy, to make sure that she was at hand if there were an emergency. She couldn't get to the hospital quickly enough.

Michael Vane watched her drive off.

He was aware of a watching man at the back and front; probably there were others whom he could not see in any case, there was nothing he could do about it. He went into the living-room. There was an eerie quiet about a house in the small hours, and he had never been more aware of it than now. He filled and lit his pipe, and sat back in an easy chair with his legs up on another, and within hand's reach of the telephone; he would wake at the first ring. He felt exhausted, and realised that it would serve no purpose to stay awake for the sake of it.

He put out the main light, left on a table lamp, and began to doze.

He woke when a car engine sounded outside, and in a moment he was on his feet. He saw a man loom up in the headlamps of the car as it slowed down. He hurried to the front door as the driver got out, and he saw that it was Mannering. He drew aside to let him enter, and closed the door. He felt a fierce hope, that Mannering had news.

"Did your wife go out alone?" Mannering asked.
"Yes. Why——"
The glint in Mannering's eyes suggested excitement more than foreboding, and there was eagerness in his manner as he said;

"Speak quite normally and don't exclaim. I think someone's up in your loft. Did you know?"

CHAPTER TEN

HIDING PLACE

MANNERING saw Vane's lips form the word '*what*' and then saw him check himself and turn his head towards the kitchen. The loft hatch was in a corner of the kitchen, close to the small passage which led up to a bathroom. A ladder, pulled by a pulley and rope, was in position by the side of the wall. A chair stood by it, too; the one with the footmarks on the seat.

"What makes you think anyone's up there?" Vane asked, whispering.

"I'm pretty sure that I saw someone looking down at us," Mannering said.

"Who——"

"We'll find out," Mannering said, "but I don't want the police to know, yet. Make sure they haven't closed in, will you?"

"Yes," Vane said. Mannering watched him go, then stepped into the kitchen. The curtains were drawn, and there was no risk of anyone seeing in. He opened the back door, and saw and heard no one; the police were watching from some distance off, and were taking no notice of him. He closed and locked the door, and glanced up at the loft hatch, without making that too noticeable. It did not fit flush against the frame, a fact which he had noticed after seeing the little patch of mud, with a few bits of grass, on the seat of the chair by the wall.

Vane came back.

"There are two of them further along the road."

"That's all right," Mannering said. "We'll keep our voices low." He pointed to the mud and the grass, and then to a mark on the wall, as if someone had drawn a muddy shoe along it. Close to the hatch itself there was the clear impression of finger prints.

Vane whispered: "*Hester!*"

"Go up and see."

Vane said: "I can't believe it." There was radiance in his eyes when he stepped towards the chair, climbed up on it, and placed the flat of his hand against the wooden hatch, and eased it up more. "*Hester!*" he whispered. "Are you there?"

Mannering held his breath, fearful that he was wrong. There was a long pause before Vane called again, more loudly:

"*Hester!*"

Mannering heard the girl answer, also in a whisper, heard the slight movement as she came across the loft towards the hatch.

"Thank God you're safe!" Vane exclaimed, and his voice was too loud. "Thank God——"

"*Quiet*," breathed Mannering.

Vane caught his breath, and whispered: "Hester, are you all right?" He was pushing the hatch further back, and now the girl appeared, looking rather like a sprite, auburn hair bared and loose. She was on her knees by the side of the hatch, and her eyes seemed very bright.

"Hal—hallo, Dad."

"*Are you all right?*"

"Yes, I—I'm not hurt."

"Come down, and——"

"If she comes down we've got to make sure she doesn't leave any tell-tale signs behind," Mannering said.

"That's all right, I'll lift her."

"Her shadow mustn't appear against the windows," Mannering went on, urgently. "If the police think that she's here they'll close in at once."

"She can't stay there," Vane protested.

"I could," Hester whispered.

"Lift her down, and stay in the kitchen," Mannering said. "Hungry, Hester?"

She sounded almost like a little girl.

"I am, rather."

Mannering watched as Vane stood beneath the hatch, on the chair, and his daughter sat on the side, her legs dangling, and then edged herself downwards. Her father took her weight, with his hands at her waist. He lowered her until she was standing in front of him, and they were gripping hands. The girl wore the dark green duffle coat, which might look blue in some lights. Her hair was rumpled, her stockings laddered, her shoes covered with mud and pieces of last autumn's leaves. Mannering gave them a full minute, and then asked:

"How long have you been there?"

"I came in while the police were here," Hester answered.

"*While* they were here?" exclaimed Vane.

"You and Mr. Hennessy were talking in the front room."

"Good Lord!" Vane exclaimed. "You must——" he didn't finish. "*Are* you all right?"

Hester was looking at Mannering now.

"Yes," she answered, "but I'm scared."

"I'll bet you are!" said her father.

"Let's deal with this appetite first," Mannering said, and turned towards the larder. "Keep to the other side of the room, Hester, don't stand or pass between the light and the window."

"All right."

"What happened?" her father demanded.

She didn't answer.

Mannering said: "I'll make a guess. You were with Clive Morgan, who was demanding more money, and you told him you couldn't find it for him. You left him sitting in the car. Soon afterwards you went back, and found him dead. You were so frightened that you just ran away—into the woods. You were there when the police arrived, you knew they would soon start looking for you, and—that frightened you even more."

"Yes, that's all true," Hester said. She had fine, honey-coloured eyes. "I—I've never been so scared. Dad, I didn't kill him."

"Of course you didn't!"

"The police think I did."

"The police can be fools," Vane said, sharply. "Darling, why didn't you come down when the police had gone?"

Again she didn't answer.

"Hester, you must tell me——"

"Where's Mother?" Hester asked suddenly, as if she was determined not to answer that particular question.

Then she looked aghast at the change in her father's expression. Until that moment, Mannering realised, Vane had forgotten his son; excitement and relief at finding his daughter had driven the other anxiety away.

"Dad, what is it?" The girl was suddenly alarmed. "Mother's all right, isn't she?"

"Your mother's all right," Mannering said, "but your brother's been injured, and he's been taken to hospital. Your mother has gone to see him."

Hester backed away, losing all her colour. Then she poured out a torrent of questions about Guy, and her affection for her brother became vividly alive.

When she knew what there was to know, Mannering pulled up a chair and helped her to sit down. She was so white that it looked as if she would faint. He put on a kettle and foraged in the larder, leaving father and daughter facing each other, silent for what seemed a long time, then suddenly beginning to talk at once. If Vane had any sense he would let the truth pour out of the girl. He tried to catch Vane's eye, but that wasn't necessary. Hester was now talking very quickly.

Morgan had wanted more money, and made her promise to meet him at the Hall gates that night. She had pleaded with him for a long time, but had left him when he had started to become unpleasant. She had got lost, seen the side lights of his car and gone back to see him dead; that much she had already said. Then she had come home, walking across country, frightened, until she had reached the bungalow and seen the police car outside; she had recognised it as Hennessy's. No one else had been about. She had come in the back way. The back door had been locked, but there was a key outside. She had felt nervous as well as frightened, the quarrel with her mother had weighed heavily on her mind, she wasn't sure what kind of reception she would get. She had crept to the living-room, heard Hennessy talking, and realised just what her danger was. She had feared that Hennessy would want to take her away, and had climbed up to the loft.

"I just didn't know what to do when the police went," she said. "Dad, I'm terribly sorry, but I didn't know what to do. I suppose I was so hungry and tired, I couldn't see anything straight. I was afraid that Mother would be angry, that when you knew I'd taken the money you would be, too. I just felt that I couldn't face you, I wanted to be on my own. And—I cried. I couldn't stop myself."

She was sitting very upright, by a small table with tea and sandwiches by her side; she hadn't touched a sandwich yet, all she wanted was to talk.

"There's an old mattress up there," she went on. "I lay on it, and sobbed and—well, I must have dropped asleep, and woke up and heard voices. I peeped, to see who it was. I hardly slept at all last night, I haven't been sleeping on Thursdays for weeks because I hated taking the money, but—I had to take it."

"*Don't ask her why*," Mannering pleaded silently.

Vane said: "Coming here was the best thing you could have done. Whatever the trouble is, we'll see you through it. If you hadn't been so tired you would have known that all the time."

She nodded, gratefully.

"Now eat one of those sandwiches," Vane ordered and looked at Mannering. "Mr. Mannering——"

Hester exclaimed: "*Who?*"

"John Mannering," her father explained.

Hester looked at Mannering as if at a freak. A sandwich was half-way to her mouth, her eyes were open to their widest. Vane showed his remarkable capacity for saying nothing at the right time, and Mannering waited, too.

"*You're* the reason that Clive wanted more money! He said he had to have four weeks—four weeks' pay in advance, he wanted to go away while you were at the Hall. He thought you might recognise him."

"Good God!" exclaimed Vane.

"Did you recognise him?" demanded Hester.

"As a blackmailer, yes," Mannering answered. "He blackmailed some friends of mine, years ago. The police didn't know. So he wanted to hide for a few weeks, did he?"

"That's what he said, and that's why it was impossible to—to pay him."

Here was the moment.

"Pay him for what?" asked Mannering.

He knew that she wasn't going to answer, saw the way her lips tightened and the determination showed in her eyes. She was so tired; drawn; frightened. The accumulation of weeks of anxiety and worry crowded upon her, but she had one secret which she intended to keep.

"I can't tell you," she said and turned to her father. "Dad, I hate myself for what I've done, but I can't tell you. I just can't. Don't try to make me. Don't—don't let mother try to. That's really why I couldn't come down to see you when the police had gone. I knew you'd want to know what it was all about, and I can't tell you. I simply can't."

Vane didn't speak.

Mannering said: "No one is going to try to make you talk if you feel like that about it." Vane didn't argue or protest then, either. "We've more important things to decide, anyhow."

Vane said, with an effort: "What?"

"Are we going to hide Hester, or are we going to let the police find her?" Mannering asked, without much change of expression. "If she's under arrest the police will look after her, and they'll make sure she doesn't come to any harm. But they'll question you until you tell them everything you know. You'd have to face that."

"I wouldn't mind how much they questioned me," Hester said.

"Can we hide her?" asked Vane.

"I think we could. I'm not sure that we should," Mannering said.

"What do you recommend?"

"That when we think the moment's right, she gives herself up," Mannering answered. "It would be much more effective than if she were found by the police."

Hester said: "I suppose I ought to." She had finished one of the sandwiches, and was starting on another, eating mechanically. She had a little more colour in her cheeks, and her eyes were brighter. Mannering judged that she was genuinely calm about facing the need to give herself up; that didn't worry her. He had a feeling that she would actually be relieved when the time came.

"What would you say is the right moment?" Vane asked.

"When she's told me all that there is to tell," Mannering said.

"I can't tell anyone," Hester said, and there was no doubt at all that she meant it.

How far would Vane help with what he wanted, Mannering wondered. How deep did his understanding go? He must know that his daughter would not talk to him or her mother; here was something which she was desperately anxious not to discuss with her parents. She might discuss it with him; or he might be able to jolt her sufficiently to make her talk. If he asked Vane to go, now, though the reason would be too obvious, and might even strengthen the girl's obstinacy.

Mannering said: "I'm probably talking out of turn, but if your wife comes back while Hester's here, it's going to be extremely difficult."

"It is."

"She'll try to make me talk, and I simply can't," Hester said dismally.

"The best thing might be for Hester to come away with me, and when a chance comes, to give herself up to the police," suggested Mannering. "They'll certainly take her into custody, and I shouldn't think they'll release her for at least eight days— there would be a first hearing and a remand in custody. In those eight days, a lot might resolve itself."

"I think you're probably right." There was disquiet in Vane's eyes because of the deception he would have to practise on his wife, but he faced up to that as he did to most things. "But how can you get Hester away?"

"We'll have to use our wits," Mannering said. "The police will be watching for her coming in, they won't expect her to go out." He grinned suddenly, to give them heart, and saw the girl respond. "Willing to come with me, Hester?"

"Yes."

"I like this family," Mannering declared. "I only hope I can make it like me! I've Guy's bicycle in the boot of the car, which is backing on to your drive now. I'll cause a distraction, and if Hester hides her face and walks just in front of you, Vane, the police won't see her, even if they aren't fooled by me. You take out the bicycle. While you're wheeling it away, Hester can climb in the boot. There's plenty of room."

Hester's eyes lit up.

Vane said: "Where do you intend to take her?"

"Wouldn't it be better if you didn't know, so that you honestly can't tell the police?" suggested Mannering. Before Vane had time to think, he stood up, and went on: "The quicker we're off the better. Bury your head in that big collar, Hester, and keep your hands in your pocket. This is what I'll do. . . ."

CHAPTER ELEVEN

CAR RIDE

HESTER saw the pale light of the stars, the shape of the rooftop of the house opposite, the black outline of Mannering's car, and the shape of her father's figure. She had never felt more conspicuous. She walked a step in front of her father, and he kept touching the back of her foot with his toes; any moment she was afraid that she might stumble, and knew that he was so desperately anxious to make sure that no one saw her. Mannering had crossed the back garden and was to distract the police, further along the street, but a man appeared, on the right.

He drew nearer.

He did not speak, and in the dim light he looked massive. He wore a trilby hat, adding to his height, and his footsteps were heavy but clear. She was sure that this was a policeman; one of the watching men. She could see the outline of his body clearly. She had a scarf wound about her face so that only her eyes were uncovered, and her own breath was hot against the silk, but she felt sure she would be seen.

The man stopped.

Her father kicked her heel and she almost stumbled.

Then there was a crash of breaking glass further along the street, shattering the night's quiet.

The man spun round, and Hester saw her father dart forward to the car. He lifted the bicycle out as footsteps sounded along the street. The big man shouted: "Stop there!" and gave chase.

Hester felt enormous relief, and yet was weak from reaction. There was a light inside the boot lid, showing the huge boot, a few tools, a flashlight and a tennis racquet. She scrambled in. The footsteps had almost stopped, now; then the big man came hurrying back.

"The devil got away," he said gruffly. "It wasn't your daughter, was it?"

"Don't be silly," Vane said. "That was a man." As he spoke, Mannering appeared from the side of the house, and he was not even breathing hard.

"Didn't I hear a smash?" he asked.

"Someone broke a window," the big man said, and almost on his words a light went on further along the street where a neighbour had been disturbed.

Mannering said: "Got the bicycle out, Mr. Vane?"

"Yes."

"Then I'll be off," Mannering said.

There was plenty of room for Hester to squat, but as the lid came down, the light went out. Suddenly it was pitch dark, and seemed like being shut up in a black hole. The top pressed lightly against Hester's head, and she bent down further, straining her neck. She heard the snap of the fastener, yet still dared hardly breathe, as if fearful that she would be heard. There were footsteps and the sound of voices, then a movement as if the car were swaying. Mannering was getting in. She breathed more freely now, and wriggled to and fro, to get more comfortable. There was a sharp movement, as if the whole car shook for a moment, then a steady vibration: the engine was turning. A door slammed. She heard the wheels on the gravel of the drive, felt herself thrust to one side as the car turned out of the drive and on to the road. If the detective had not moved, he must be within hands' reach of her now.

The car straightened, and she felt it surge forward, the vibration softer. There was a long, swaying motion but no bumping. After the first few seconds she felt a great sense of relief, and moved again; she could sit nearly upright, hugging her knees and bending her head so that her chin was on her chest. She felt the car swing at the curves, but no longer had any sense of alarm.

Then the car slowed down, and alarm flared up again.

Was someone stopping it? Was there a policeman, searching all cars? Everything she had heard about a police hunt sprang into her mind.

The car stopped, she sensed movement, and the next moment the boot opened and the greyness of the starlight came in.

"All right?" asked Mannering, in a whisper.

"Yes, thank you."

"When I get to the Hall I may leave you there, and come back for you. The night watchman may be resting between rounds."

"All right."

"You'll do," Mannering said.

She just made out the gleam of his teeth. Then he closed the boot, and all the now familiar sounds and movements were repeated. He drove more swiftly, and the road seemed very smooth. Suddenly Hester was thrust against the side, at a sharp left turn; they had entered the gateway of the Hall. She did not know that there were still policemen on duty, two police cars nearby, and among the woods, men searching with lanterns and torches, and beating the undergrowth with their sticks.

The car stopped again.

She heard a murmur of voices, and felt panic greater than any she had ever known. It was like a torment inside her. If the police had insisted on opening the boot, if they found her, she would be taken to the police station, charged, kept in a cell—

The car went on.

She closed her eyes, and prayed that she would not have to wait in the boot for long; she would know terror every minute of the time. The car swung right and left along the drive, then the road straightened out, and she knew exactly where she was. When they stopped again, she strained her ears to catch the sound of voices, but heard none. Her heart began to pound. Would Mannering let her out at once, or was she doomed to spend a long time here?

She heard footsteps; then silence fell.

What would happen if someone came and found her here before Mannering returned?

She had waited up in the loft, for so long; she had lived on the edge of fear for so long, too. She couldn't stand much more waiting. She felt as if she would suffocate, it was so stuffy and hot. *She must get out.* She couldn't breathe, it wasn't any use pretending; she couldn't stay in here. She pushed at the boot, but it would not open. In sudden panic she pushed again and tried to thump on it with her clenched fist, but she only hurt her knuckles.

I must keep still, she told herself.

The night watchman might have heard her already; if she were found now, it would be her own fault. She clenched her teeth in an effort to make up for what she had already done, but it was no use, she couldn't sit cramped up here any longer, she would have to get out somehow.

She would have to scream.

There were footsteps.

If this was Mannering, he must let her out, she couldn't stay here for another minute. But if it wasn't Mannering, what would she do? One cry, and whoever was coming would hear.

The footsteps were very close; someone was approaching the boot, obviously coming straight to it. She did not think it was Mannering. Now she bit her lips and tried to stop breathing for fear of making sound, and there was no calm in her.

The boot opened, and a man stood looking at her in the garage light.

It was Rodney Horton, who was smiling at her in a

tense kind of way; and then suddenly moved, to help her. As she got out and stood up, he held her very close, arms tight about her. And she found herself sobbing from this shock of surprise.

"Rod, oh, Rod."

"It's all right," Rodney Horton soothed. "It's all right. You needn't worry, darling, you needn't worry at all."

Mannering heard him say that.

Mannering was standing in a corner of the garage, unseen by either of them. Although the light was on, the watchman was on his rounds, and he had met Rodney, Lord Horton's only son, in the great hall. There was both weakness and strength in Rodney, and in that moment the strength had been uppermost; he had come striding forward, gripping Mannering's arm, and asking:

"Have you heard where Hester is?"

"I know where she is," Mannering had answered.

"Is she all right?"

"Yes."

"Is she—is she under arrest?"

"No," Mannering had said, and studied the expression in his manner. "Rod, go and see if the coast is clear, will you?"

"Clear for what?" Rodney had asked.

"For Hester to come in. She's in the boot of my car."

Without wasting time the younger man had turned and hurried out of the side entrance of the Hall. Mannering had followed him to the garage, in time to see him holding Hester tightly in his arms. Mannering gave them no more than thirty seconds, and then went across.

"Sorry," he said briskly. "Rod, go and see that no one's about. Keep ahead of me all the time, and give me a warning by holding up your right hand."

"Right."

"Now," Mannering said.

Rodney turned away.

He was a stocky, fair-haired young man, and the girl was about the same height. He had rugged good looks which reminded Mannering vividly of Lord Horton. He had an unexpected grace of movement, too, but was too square-shouldered and broad across the hips for his height.

He disappeared.

"Come on," Mannering said to Hester, and took her arm. He had a curiously impersonal manner whenever he wanted to adopt it, and he did now. He led her along a passage towards a small courtyard where two lights burned at narrow windows, swept her across a grass lawn, and into the arched doorway at the side of the Hall. There was a wide brick-walled passage with a few paintings on the walls, and a great iron studded door at the end. Mannering opened this, peered round it, and then ushered the girl into the main hall. Instead of going to the great staircase, he crossed to another door, like this, where Rodney was standing. Beyond was a spiral staircase, chill and bleak, its stone treads worn with the feet of centuries. Mannering helped the girl up, until they came to a wide passage with several doors leading off. Rodney Horton stood at one of the doors, beckoning.

Mannering crossed with the girl, and ushered her inside. The door closed, and Rodney stood leaning against it, looking at her.

Mannering was sure of one thing: in spite of her danger, in spite of the suspicions of the police, in spite of what had just happened, these two young people were oblivious of him: no one mattered to either, but the other. It was a complete absorption seldom seen, and he found himself smiling faintly.

This was his sitting-room; next to it was his bedroom, next to that, his bathroom. Each was a high room, furnished in Jacobean furniture which had a dull lustre. The furniture and the room dwarfed the three people in it, and Mannering saw that Rodney was in fact an inch shorter than the girl.

He said: "Very interesting. How long has this been going on?"

Rodney started, and turned round to him.

"What?"

"This romance. Isn't that the word?"

"Romance," Rodney almost choked.

"How long?" asked Mannering.

"We—we've known each other for about three months," said Rodney. "Any objection?"

"Does your father know?"

"No, but when the time comes I'll tell him."

"Sure he doesn't know?"

"Of course I'm sure." Rodney's voice took on an overtone of impatience. "What difference does it make, anyhow? The only thing that matters is hiding Hester."

"I'm not so sure," Mannering said, mildly. "I think a lot of other things are equally important. Making sure she doesn't come to any harm, for instance, and so finding out who really killed Clive Morgan."

"The police are bound to find the murderer——" Rodney began, but Mannering cut him short with a gesture, and both Rodney and Hester looked at him with a kind of fear.

"I shouldn't leave it to the police, they may not know all the facts," Mannering went on. "I do know some of those facts. I think this is a moment to think about the implications." He moved forward, took the girl's arm and led her into the inner room, waited until she sat in a tall backed winged armchair, which faced the great stone fireplace. Rodney stood by her side, wary, one arm raised and bent, as if ready for instant action if any threat materialised. He looked very young; younger than his twenty-three years.

"Now what's on your mind?" he demanded.

"Just this," answered Mannering promptly. "You and Hester have known each other for about three months. Hester has been blackmailed for about eight weeks. Hester refused to tell her father why she had been blackmailed. Has it anything to do with her association with you?"

Before either of them spoke, he felt sure that he was right.

The only doubt was whether they would confide in him.

CHAPTER TWELVE

TRUTH?

MANNERING watched the girl more closely than he watched Rodney. Hester was an easier subject to assess, and much less practised in deceit; the boy had been forced into deceitfulness most of his life. Mannering knew his history better than most, and the only thing he could not be sure about was how his upbringing had affected Rodney's mind, his character and his moods. At this moment Rodney was an aggressive, almost angry-looking youth with an out-thrust chin, his hands clenched as if he would like to come forward and use them on Mannering. In the light of the room, his eyes seemed a silvery grey colour.

The girl was—frightened.

Rodney spoke at last, in a voice which almost grated.

"What are you trying to say? That *I'm* blackmailing the girl I love?"

"Clive Morgan did the blackmailing," Mannering said, "but it could have been because of something he knew about you. Hester, it's time you told me exactly what this is about. You have my word that I won't tell your parents without your permission, but I must know what hold Morgan was able to exert over you."

The girl didn't answer.

Mannering had seen how adamant she could be when she had been in her own home, and that hadn't changed. The whole of the Vane bungalow would stand inside this suite of rooms, he knew, yet the girl seemed to fit into both backgrounds. In spite of the blue-green duffle coat threads, pulled with thorns, her ruffled hair and her tired eyes, there was real quality about her.

"Better tell me than the police," he said.

"The police don't come into it," Rodney declared, sharply.

"They will if I call them in."

"What the devil do you mean?"

"Rodney, you're heading for trouble with everyone if you go on behaving like this," Mannering said, deceptively mild. "Shake out of it. Hester's wanted by the police. I've brought her here to find out what she had to say, and if it's reasonable, I'll try to help her. If it isn't, I'll tell the police where to find her."

"The mistake you made was in letting me know she was here, at all," Rodney said, with a note of anger in his voice. "If Hester doesn't want to talk, you're not going to make her."

"Aren't I?" asked Mannering, almost musingly. "Hester, you have exactly five minutes. In that time you'll have told me what Morgan had against you, or I shall call the police. I'd be happier if you were in the police station, anyhow; you'd be safer."

Rodney snapped: "What do you mean, safer?"

"She appears to have been cleverly framed for a vicious murder," Mannering pointed out, his voice still low-pitched. "And a little later her brother was savagely attacked." He saw the pain in the girl's eyes at that reminder, but gave her no opportunity to dwell on it as he went on: "It's obvious that the two things might be connected, and I don't want Hester attacked. Hester—what did Morgan know that made him able to blackmail you?"

"Can't you see she's tired out?" demanded Rodney hotly. "Can't you at least have the decency to let her have a few hours' rest? In the morning——"

"One minute's gone," Mannering said.

"Damn you, she doesn't have to tell you or anyone!"

"Either she tells me or the police will come for her, and they won't take very long, there are some at the

TRUTH?

foot of the drive." When neither of them answered, Mannering went on much more sharply: "I don't know what the pair of you think you're up to. I persuaded Mr. Vane to tell me all he knew. It was bad enough before when Hester was actually stealing from her own father in order to pay Morgan, but now——"

Rodney exclaimed: "*What?*" He took a step forward, as if he would like to choke Mannering, then turned and looked at the girl he claimed to love. She was sitting bolt upright, and didn't speak; no one could doubt that she was admitting the truth of what Mannering had said, and that she did not know how Rod would receive it.

"You robbed your father," Rodney breathed.

Hester raised her head, hopelessly.

"Rod, I—I had to get the money, I simply had to. Morgan—Morgan asked for more than you were able to give me. I had to get it from somewhere."

Rodney's eyes seemed to burn in that pale face, and the aggressive thrust of his chin was more marked than before.

"My God," he said, as if aghast. "And you didn't tell me."

"You had enough worries already."

"When are you going to learn that you come first, all the time, in my life?" Rodney strode towards her, gripped her shoulders, and made Mannering think that he was actually hurting the girl. "You've done far more than your share in trying to protect me and in trying to protect my father. You come first, understand, and the rest nowhere. How long has this been going on?"

Hester said: "Nine weeks, altogether."

But there was a change in her. Fear had gone, or at least had faded. Tiredness had faded, too. Her eyes glowed with a new kind of radiance, and Mannering could not fail to see that as she looked up into the face of the younger man. They were silent for a moment, and then Rodney moved his hands, took Hester's arms and drew her to her feet. The way in which he could forget Mannering's presence was quite remarkable.

Too remarkable?

Mannering said: "So she was protecting you, and you let her do it?"

Rodney swung round.

"I don't like that insinuation."

"Is it insinuation or fact?"

"Rod, we're going to need help to get out of this mess," Hester said, "and Mr. Mannering's done a great deal already. We ought——"

"There's just one thing you don't know about John Mannering," Rodney interrupted, and made the words almost sneer. "He's a close friend of my father. I don't know what he's doing down here, but he's snooping for some reason—probably snooping into my life."

"Rod——" the girl began, unhappily.

Mannering said: "You ought to be careful with this young man, Hester. People who are fond of him get into serious trouble. His father——"

"My father hates the sight of me!" Rodney burst out. "You know he does."

"I know that I could understand it if he did," Mannering said, almost amiably. "Hester, did Morgan threaten to disclose your association with Rodney unless you paid him money?" He paused, to judge the reaction, and knew that he was only partly right, for Hester's eyes flickered a message to Rodney. "Come on, is that it?"

"Partly."

"Hester you don't have to tell Mannering a thing!" Rodney almost shouted.

"You could tell me yourself, couldn't you?" Mannering said. "Isn't it a fact that Morgan knew something else about you and threatened disclosure? You were so anxious to keep it quiet that you used Hester as a go-between. Morgan told you he wanted so much a week and actually squeezed more from her. How much did you pay him?"

"It's no business of ——" Rodney began.

Mannering said roughly: "Please yourself, but if you haven't told me everything you can by the time I've reached that telephone, I shall call the police. I'm sick and tired of you throwing your weight about, getting other people into trouble, hiding your own nasty little secret." He strode towards a telephone in a corner of the room, and the girl watched him, scared. It looked as if Rodney would fling himself forward, to stop Mannering.

The girl cried: "Don't I—I paid Morgan forty pounds every week. Rodney gave me fifteen of it, that's the amount Morgan had told him, and I knew Rodney was in difficulties over money. I—I tried to help him."

"Sure he deserved it?"

"What makes you talk like that?" demanded the girl, and there was a kind of anguish in her eyes. "Why do you two dislike each other so much?"

"I dislike any man who hides behind a girl."

"I didn't know——" Rodney began.

"You knew that Hester was seeing Morgan for you. You knew he was vicious and money-grabbing, but rather than be seen with him yourself, you let Hester meet him. How much of a hero does that make you?"

"I wanted to help!" Hester cried. "It wasn't Rodney's fault, I suggested helping, I insisted on seeing Morgan. I didn't think it would do me any harm."

"It's put you on the run from a charge of murder," Mannering said, acidly. "Rodney, let's have the truth. What did Morgan have on you?"

Rodney was standing absolutely still, very pale again, and his eyes glittering; but he was not the furious youth of a few minutes before. Something that the girl had said had affected him, probably he realised the full enormity of the risk he had allowed her to take.

He said: "All right, Mannering, I'll tell you. Hester—Hester doesn't know everything. She simply knew that Morgan was able to blackmail me. But it's time she knew more."

"You don't have to tell me," Hester declared, and turned towards the door.

"Don't run away from this, too," Mannering said sharply.

Rodney said: "You don't like us at all, Mannering, do you? You'll like me even less when you've heard this. My father has a large number of old masters and precious *objets d'art* and valuable antiques at the Hall. He also keeps me on a chain. I am allowed a beggarly sum of money every month, I can't do a thing I want to do, I can't even marry the girl I love. All the family money is entailed. He behaves as if I'm a puppet on the end of a string. Like him? I hate the sight of him and all he stands for! And everything in this house—everything—will be mine if I outlive him, and there's no reason why I shouldn't. So I sold some of the *objets d'art* and replaced them with replicas. Morgan is a jewel-smith who made the replicas for me, and when he realised what I was doing, he began to blackmail me. That's all there is to it." Rodney squared his shoulders and stared defiantly at Mannering, but he was more conscious of the way the girl was looking at him. There was no doubt that he had hated making the admission, and did not want to summon the courage to look at her. It wasn't possible to guess what was in her mind.

"How long have you been doing this?" asked Mannering.

"For a year or so."

"How long has Morgan been in it?"

"Almost from the beginning. I met him when some pieces of jade were broken, and I took them to him for repair. He worked for an old man who died a year ago, leaving Morgan the business. The blackmail started about three months ago. He telephoned me first, and then came to see me. I couldn't let him come here and I didn't want to meet him outside, so——" now Rodney looked at Hester. "You ought to say it," he growled. "I'm all kinds of a swine, and Mannering's quite right, I ought to be horsewhipped. But if you knew how I hate——"

"Don't say you hate your father again, Rod," Hester said, unexpectedly calm and quiet-voiced. "I knew you were in difficulties and wanted to help you. I'm glad I did. How—how serious is it, Mr. Mannering? Can we tell Lord Horton now, and clear the air?"

"I think he'd have me sent to jail," Rodney put in bitterly. "You ought to know, Mannering. You're down here because he hired you to find out what was happening to the things that were missing, didn't he? You've been surveying all the priceless junk in the hall, telling him which is real and which is false. And you know what he will do when he realises who's behind it."

Mannering said: "He knows. He also knew you were being blackmailed. He thinks that Morgan worked for someone else—someone to whom he sold everything you took." Mannering paused, seeing the astonishment in Rodney's face, and then went on: "But that isn't the important factor now."

"Then what is?" demanded Rodney.

Mannering went to the girl's side and rested a hand on her shoulder.

"This is," he said. "While Morgan was alive you were in acute danger of being found out, and that terrified you. You believed your father would cut your allowance right out, and might even make an example of you by having you charged with theft. You had as good a reason as any man could have to want Morgan dead."

Hester held her breath.

"Did you kill him?" Mannering demanded.

CHAPTER THIRTEEN

SECOND HIDING PLACE

MANNERING was ready for any reaction, and would not have been surprised if, after the first shock of the question, Horton's son completely lost his self-control. Rodney stood quite still for what seemed a long time. Mannering glanced at Hester, seeing the tension with which she watched the man for whom she had made such sacrifices. It was almost as if she was frightened in case Horton had killed the blackmailer; as if she believed that he had.

Still Rodney stood quite motionless.

"Rod——" Hester began, but broke off.

Mannering didn't speak.

Rodney raised his right hand, very slowly, touched his chin, and began to rub with thumb and forefinger. His eyes glittered, but there was no hint of a physical storm.

"No, Mannering, I didn't," he answered. He looked at Hester. "I would have killed Morgan soon enough if I'd had the chance and could have got away with it. Devils like that don't deserve to live. But I would give my life to save Hester's. I wouldn't risk hers."

That sounded so simple that it seemed almost naïve. Hester moved towards Rodney, and he put his right arm round her waist; but there was no passion in his voice or his embrace.

"You took a long time answering," Mannering said.

Rodney made no comment.

"Mr. Mannering, can't you——" Hester began.

Rodney said: "We've got to work this out, Hester. I took a long time answering because two things jolted me badly. I don't know whether my father knew or not, but if he did and didn't tell me, he must have some fiendish punishment in store. The other thing's far more important. It didn't occur to me that anyone might think I'd kill Morgan and let you take the blame. They don't know how I feel about you. But I was down by the gates."

Hester exclaimed: "Rod, you needn't tell——"

"I wasn't happy about the situation, and I watched out for Morgan," Rodney went on, grimly. "I had two of the gardeners looking out for him, too, and one of them told me he was by the gates in his car. What was he doing—stepping up the pressure?"

"He wanted twice as much money," Hester said, and coloured slightly as she added: "Or payment in kind."

"I had a nasty feeling it was something like that," Rodney said. "Well, I went down to see him on my motor-cycle. I heard his car turn off the road a hundred yards away and I thought that he was going to walk up to the house, so I went to look for him."

"Did you see him?" Mannering asked.

Rodney answered slowly: "I saw him sitting in the car with Hester. I didn't interrupt them. Then he and Hester had a row, and she went off. I was afraid she might be lost in the woods, and followed her." He broke off, pressing his right hand against his forehead. "I'd better tell the whole truth now, Hester. I'm all kinds of a swine and the only point of view I really see is my own. Instead of going and breaking Morgan's neck, I went after you to find out what he was asking for now. I was terrified in case I couldn't keep him quiet. I knew that if I saw him he'd round on me, because of the way you'd talked to him."

"Did you two meet?" Mannering demanded.

"Yes," Rodney answered. "We talked for ten minutes, but Hester only told me about the higher price Morgan wanted. She persuaded me that I ought to get back to the Hall. I told myself she was right. I'm just beginning to see myself as other people see me,

Mannering. The hell of it is, I can't undo that now, but I can make sure that I don't hide behind Hester or anyone else in the future. And there's one way that will take the heat off." He gave a fierce, unexpected grin. "Isn't that the right phrase?"

"How?" demanded Mannering.

"I can say that I was down by the car, and that I'm just as much a suspect as she is."

"That won't help," Hester exclaimed.

Mannering said: "It might help, but we want to time it properly. Did you see anyone else near the car?"

"No."

"Did you?" Mannering asked the girl.

"No."

"All right." Mannering became more brisk. "Rodney, is it still fairly easy to reach the old tower room?"

"Yes, I use it a lot."

"That's the best place for Hester to hide for the time being," Mannering said. "We can get her up there without anyone seeing, and you can take food up to her during the day and see that she has everything she needs. Is anyone else about, do you know?"

"Shouldn't think so," Rodney said.

"Go and make sure, will you?"

"Right." Rodney gave Hester a squeeze, and then went into the other room, and into the hall. The girl stood looking silently at Mannering.

"I want you to stay in the tower room until I come and see you myself," Mannering said. "Don't leave it for any other reason. Don't leave it even if Rodney tells you to: his judgement isn't sound. It was once a kind of strong-room. The previous Lord Horton kept most of his valuables and pictures up there, but since another strong-room was built underground, it hasn't been used much. It's a kind of tower wing, above the observation balcony, and provided no one sees you, it's the last place anyone will think of looking for you."

"I'll stay there," Hester decided, and asked very quietly: "You don't think Rodney killed Morgan, do you?"

"I simply don't know," Mannering answered. "But I don't think it's likely."

Hester didn't speak.

"Before he comes back, there's one other thing I want to ask," Mannering said. "Did your brother Guy know about this blackmail?"

Hester's face answered him, before she said:

"Good heavens, no!"

"Could he have guessed about you and Rodney?"

"I don't think anyone could. We've always been—been so careful."

"Have you shared any confidence with him?"

"I've told you, no. Why?"

"I want to make sure that I know everything," Mannering said, and then the door opened and Rodney called in a low-pitched voice:

"All clear."

"Come on," said Mannering.

He knew the way up to the tower room almost as well as Rodney, for he had often visited this house at a time when the room had been used as a gallery for the pictures, the antiques and the *objets d'art* with which this great house was filled. He had been there several times a year, sometimes to admire, sometimes to value new pieces bought by the old Lord Horton.

They walked round the gallery, looking down into the great hall, then through an arched doorway and up another flight of spiral steps. It struck very cold. They crossed another hallway, and stepped into a small lift, which looked like an ordinary doorway from the outside. It went up slowly, all three were pressed closely together in the small car. When it stopped, Rodney opened the doors and they stepped on to a small landing. Two windows were almost opposite it, and a doorway leading, as Mannering knew, to a balcony which commanded magnificent views over the countryside towards Gilston and the south-west. Through the windows, on either side of this door, the lights of Gilston showed. This was as far as anyone came, as a rule. Opposite the lift was a narrow doorway leading to another spiral staircase, even narrower than the first; and it ended a dozen steps up in a blank stone wall.

Rodney inserted a key in a keyhole that Mannering could not see, then pressed against one of the great blocks of stone. There was a slight whirring sound, and the 'wall' blocking the stairway began to turn.

"At one time there was a guard at every doorway up here," no one could get past here without being questioned by at least four people."

Hester said: "I see."

The 'wall' had swung round so that they could squeeze through to the continuation of the staircase. Rodney led the way, Hester followed, with Mannering just behind her. He held her arms as they went up. He could tell that she was edgy and nervous; and the tower was enough to scare any woman. He wondered whether she would be able to face it out alone, whether she would say that she could not go on with it.

She did not.

Then they stepped into the first of three rooms, a small one, with some old-fashioned armchairs, a couch, blankets, rugs, a radio on a small table, a record-player. The girl was so surprised that she stopped on the threshold.

"I use this as a kind of funk-hole," Rodney explained. "When I really find the others unbearable, I say I'm going away for a day or two, and come up here. There's a bathroom and bedroom—the strong-room guards used to live here, and it's as cosy as a flat in Knightsbridge. You can see all over the park by day, and it's like being in an eyrie—you're right up here in the sky with the eagles and the aeroplanes. You'll love it," Rodney added, and then looked at Mannering and gave a twisted grin. "I'm going to stay up here for a while, and I don't mean what your suspicious mind thinks I mean."

"If I thought you did, I'd have the police here in ten minutes," Mannering said. "Have you a spare key?"

"Yes."

"Then let me have yours and you use the spare one, will you?"

Rodney hesitated, then shrugged and handed a long, thin key over. Mannering put this in his pocket, as he turned to the girl. "Hester, I'll look after your mother and father, and I'll do everything I can to find the man who murdered Morgan. Have you now told me everything?"

"Yes," she answered simply.

"Fine! Rodney, how many things have you kept back?"

"I forgot to tell you the fiendish devices that my dear father has developed to keep me short of money and always ready to come to heel. He seems to think that I ought to be a kind of whipping-boy. If you want my opinion, he's got a warped mind. All the treasures here have turned him into a kind of Shylock."

"What is the value of the things you've taken and sold?"

"Upwards of two thousand pounds, I suppose."

"Is that the lot?"

"Isn't it enough?"

"It'll do to be going on with," Mannering agreed. "I'll see you about midday, Rodney. Good night." He smiled at the girl, then turned and went carefully down the cold staircase, to the landing, to the lift, then along the gallery until he reached his own room. He watched every step he took; watched every corner and every piece of furniture that was large enough to hide a man. He saw and heard nothing, but there was eeriness in this great house, heightened by the visit to the tower room.

He retraced his steps, going right up to the blocked spiral staircase, and saw and heard no one. Now he could feel reasonably sure that they had not been seen. He undressed, and got into bed, very tired now that the need for concentrated thought was over. One phrase kept coming back into his mind.

"Is that the lot?" he had asked Rodney.

"Isn't that enough?" Rodney had retorted.

It might seem plenty; two thousand pounds was still a lot of money even these days. But Mannering was here to investigate the loss of nearer two hundred thousand pounds' worth of paintings and *objets d'art*.

Horton suspected his son of stealing these, under pressure, and knew that Rodney had taken some.

Had Rodney tried to pull the wool over his, Mannering's eyes, or was there someone else doing the same thing as he had done on a much larger scale? On the answer to that question rested the answers to others. Who had killed Morgan and made sure that the girl would be a suspect? And who had attacked Guy Vane?

It was after four o'clock when Mannering got into bed. He reached across to a telephone at the side of the bed, which had a direct line to the Gilston exchange, and waited a long time before a man answered:

"Give me Gilston Hospital, please," Mannering asked.

"One moment, sir."

Mannering had long enough to yawn before the hospital answered. There was another delay while inquiries were made, and then a calm voice assured him:

"Mr. Vane is no worse, sir, and is as well as can be expected. Mrs. Vane is staying here the night."

That could mean only one thing: the boy was on the danger list. His mother would be in the particular kind of despair which affected mothers in times of crisis,

SECOND HIDING PLACE 107

Vane would be alone, hardly knowing which way to turn. And it might be a long time before Guy Vane could speak and explain what had happened; even when he could do that, he might not be able to say why the attack had been made.

Mannering switched off the light, and settled down. If he could get five hours' uninterrupted sleep he would be able to cope next morning.

A knocking at the door woke Mannering, and he lay for some seconds, not sure what was happening, only knowing that he did not want to open his eyes; they seemed to be gummed down. Then the knocking was repeated. Suddenly he remembered that he had locked the door. That meant he would have to get out of bed to open it. It was broad daylight, but that meant little: it might be anything from six o'clock onwards.

"Mr. Mannering!" a man called.

Mannering made an effort. "What is it?"

"Inspector Hennessy wants to see you, sir."

"Where is he?"

"I'm here," Hennessy said in his deep voice with its unmistakable country accent. "I'm sorry to worry you, Mr. Mannering, but I must see you urgently."

Mannering called: "Wait a minute." He pushed the bedclothes back and climbed out, rubbed his eyes, yawned, and smoothed down his hair. It was sunny when he looked at the parkland of the Hall stretching out into the distance, and at tall hills beyond. He put on a dark-blue dressing-gown, and opened the bedroom door. Hennessy and a plainclothes man were standing there together with Simms, one of the Hall servants in this wing; the man who usually looked after the guests.

"I'm extremely sorry, sir," he said. "I'll bring some tea right away."

"Enough for three, please," Mannering said, and turned to Hennessy. "What's all the urgency about,

Inspector?" As he asked the question a possible explanation sprang to mind. "Is the Vane boy any worse?"

"He's still on the danger list, but I didn't come here about that, Mr. Mannering. I want to know where you took Miss Vane last night."

That question would have been bad enough coming at any time; coming now, before he was fully awake, it nearly put Mannering off his balance. He faked a yawn, smothered it, and said:

"I haven't the faintest idea where she is. What makes you think I have?"

"She was at her parents' bungalow last night, I know that now," said Hennessy. "But she isn't there this morning. She left with you. Don't say that she didn't, Mr. Mannering. Strands of a nylon stocking as well as two hairs which have been identified as Miss Vane's were found in the boot of your car. You took her away from the bungalow and hid her. I don't have to remind you that it's not safe to interfere with the police in the execution of their duty. Where is she?"

Time and time again Mannering had been challenged like this. There had been a long period when he had led a double life—as John Mannering on the one hand, and as the Baron, cracksman and jewel-thief-extraordinary on the other. The press and the public had raved over the modern Robin Hood, who robbed the rich to help the poor; and the police had set about their task of unmasking the Baron.

One man at Scotland Yard had suspected Mannering.

Hennessy spoke as if he had been fed on those deadly suspicions.

"I want your answer at once," he said coldly. "Where is Miss Vane?"

CHAPTER FOURTEEN

MANNERING BLUFFS

MANNERING looked at the block of a man in front of him as if he were astounded, and as soon as Hennessy finished, he exclaimed as if he had not heard aright:

"She was in *my* car?"

"You know very well she was!"

If Michael Vane had admitted that, lying wouldn't help, and Mannering would not even gain time; but he did not think that the market gardener would have made any admission, and felt sure that Hennessy believed in playing his trump card, in the hope of winning the game at the first round.

"I don't know anything of the kind," Mannering said. "The car was outside the bungalow while—good Lord!" He began to grin. "Are you sure of this?"

"Positive. And it's no laughing matter, Mr. Mannering."

"I think it's damned funny! The great detective, as I've been called, talking to Vane in the bungalow while the wanted daughter sneaks out and gets into the boot of my car. Have you searched the grounds?"

"All the district is being combed for her," Hennessy said. "Fifty policemen are looking for her, and at least a hundred farmworkers and estate workers. You can stop that waste of manpower, Mr. Mannering. If you don't, I can't be responsible for the consequences."

Mannering said sharply:

"I don't like threats. I don't know where the girl is. Is there anything else I can do for you, tell me, and then leave, Inspector."

Hennessy didn't speak.

The servant came back, carrying a tea tray loaded

with beautifully worked Georgian silver, and there was not only tea but wafer-thin bread-and-butter. Simms sensed the tension, put the tray down on a table, and retired to the doorway; he probably stayed near so as to hear what followed. Mannering felt the strength of Hennessy's challenge, the man was determined to flog himself so as to find the girl, probably because it would look as if he were not carrying out his duty if the suspect, daughter of a personal friend, were not soon caught. He was a simple man, he was probably a capable detective, but gave the impression that he was not used to dealing with people in this social stratum. Now that his challenge had been accepted, he did not know what to do next.

Mannering said: "How about a cup of tea, and a more rational approach to the mutual problem, Inspector?"

Hennessy said: "Well, I admit I took it for granted that you knew where Hester Vane was. I've been talking to Scotland Yard, and they——"

Mannering grinned.

"They warned you of all the villainies I can get up to, is that it?"

A reluctant smile made Hennessy look much more likeable, and he conceded:

"Well, in a way."

His companion, not the small, thin-faced man of the previous night but a larger, younger man, was smiling broadly.

"I know the Yard harbours a lot of suspicions of the tricks I play, but I'm not really as bad as that. Sit down." The police were almost now cooing doves, but Mannering warned himself that Hennessy might be pretending to be satisfied, but he thought that he had judged the man correctly from the beginning. "Shall I be mother?" The big detective sergeant positively beamed. "There's one thing you're as worried about as I am," Mannering added. He saw the look in

Hennessy's eyes, and knew that Hennessy was trying to guess what that anxiety was, so that he should not look a fool. "Why was Guy Vane attacked, and is there any connection between that and the attempt to frame his sister?"

Hennessy took it well.

"If the sister was—er—framed, sir, then it is a big question. You haven't remembered anything more about the men who attacked Guy Vane, have you?"

"No. One was short and stocky, the other taller and thin. They both wore scarves round their faces, and hats pulled down over their eyes. No indications as to who was there?"

"We've found footsteps and one or two threads of cloth on some branches and bushes," Hennessy answered, "but we can't identify either of them. There were definitely two men, you were right about that."

"When you think that someone is going to smash your head in you make sure how many there are," Mannering said dryly. "That's the crux of the whole problem, Inspector: why was Guy attacked? And what made him go into the woods when I was talking to Lord Horton?"

"We've a man sitting by the boy's bedside, we'll know the moment he comes round and we can question him," Hennessy said. He was a little overdainty in drinking tea, but his sergeant was a gusty drinker. "Mr. Mannering, will you answer one or two other questions?"

"If I can."

"What are you doing down here?"

"I thought everyone knew," said Mannering. "I'm valuing Lord Horton's collection of odds and ends."

"*Odds and ends*," breathed the sergeant.

Mannering grinned:"I suppose that was an understatement."

"Is that the real reason?" Hennessy demanded.

Mannering said: "If it isn't Lord Horton has fooled me. Anything on your mind, Inspector? I don't want to be made a fool of, and Lord Horton is a very shrewd man. You know that as well as I do."

"I don't mind admitting that we've thought for some time that something odd was happening here," Hennessy said. "We knew Morgan was a bit of a rogue, the Yard told us, and we wondered who he was after. We were never able to connect him with anyone at the Hall—until a few days ago."

Mannering kept a straight face.

"What was the connection you found then?"

"Miss Vane often met Rodney Horton on the sly," said Hennessy. "They met in Winchester or Southampton, never in Gilston. Then we realised that Morgan was probably blackmailing young Horton, using the girl as a go-between. Any reason to believe that's true, Mr. Mannering?"

"It's a possibility."

"I'll tell you what you can do for us," said Hennessy, warming up, "and that's try to find out if Lord Horton knows about his son's association with the girl. Not the kind of thing that we would expect to please his lordship! You don't need telling that a man like Lord Horton isn't the easiest to deal with, and we have to mind our p's and q's. I took a considerable chance in coming here the way I did, Mr. Mannering, but Bristow—Superintendent Bristow—of the Yard said that we needn't worry about you getting on your dignity. He said you would see me through if I made a mess of things. I wanted to ask for your help, and the best way was to make it look as if I'd come to make myself obnoxious. Anything you can find out will be very useful indeed."

"I'll see what I can find," Mannering promised, and looked into the big, broad face, wondering whether Hennessy was anything like so obvious as he looked. "Seriously—have you any idea where Hester is?"

Hennessy said: "I know what a fuss his lordship kicked up when young Mr. Rodney had an *affaire* with a chorus girl, a year ago. If it weren't for that I'd wonder if she was here. If you can put in a word, Mr. Mannering, I'd be grateful if you would warn Mr. Rodney and anyone concerned that if they try to hide anything from us, they'll only head for trouble. We have to be careful how we deal with gentry, but if they start playing ducks and drakes with the law, then they've had it. Position and money won't help them at all."

His gaze was very direct.

"I should hope not," Mannering said solemnly.

Five minutes later he shook hands with Hennessy and the big detective sergeant, and saw them out of the suite. When he went back to his bedroom he was very thoughtful indeed. Hennessy had meant that warning for him just as much as for the Hortons. But he had also meant that the girl was safe for the time being.

Mannering wondered what would be required to force Hennessy's hand and make him search the Hall.

Nothing short of another murder, probably.

Now Mannering had the two situations to face: the difficulty with the police because of the girl, and the problem of Lord Horton and the big losses at the Hall. They overlapped of course.

So did Morgan's murder.

Who had a motive for killing Morgan?

And above everything else, why had the two men been in the woods last night, the men who had viciously attacked Guy Vane and would have attacked him, Mannering, just as viciously.

Mannering looked out of the window, and saw Rodney Horton walking across one of the great lawns. That was the moment when Mannering realised how like the stocky man of the trees he was; in fact young Horton answered the description of the shorter of the two men who had attacked him and Guy Vane.

How deeply was young Horton involved?

How deeply did he hate his father?

Then Mannering saw Lord Horton appear, on horseback, from the side of the house. For a big man, he rode extremely well, and he did a great deal of riding. Now he sat, hard-faced and nearly as massive as Hennessy, trotting along a path towards his son, who stood quite still. They were two hundred yards away from Mannering, but even from here it was easy to realise that they were bitterly antagonistic; it was like two animals, sparring, hating each other. The older man took his horse closer to his son than was necessary, almost as if he meant to push Rodney out of the way. Rodney did not budge.

Mannering saw Horton's lips move, saw the red face in the bright light of the morning, and imagined he could see the sneer on the full lips.

Rodney's back was towards Mannering.

He saw the youth move, at last; he leapt at his father and struck at him. Horton seemed to be taken by surprise, and leaned back, thrusting up his hands to try to defend himself. The horse shied. Rodney struck again, and Mannering caught a glimpse of his expression, saw his lips twisted with rage, knew that he had never known an uglier relationship between father and son.

Horton was recovering, slowly.

He used his crop, and slashed it across his son's face. Rodney backed away, covering his head in turn, and Horton flung the crop at him, then kneed his horse and began to canter towards the stables at the side of the Hall. His son turned round, to stare after him. The younger man's expression was not good to see.

Mannering said: "I'd like to know what that was all about."

He bathed and shaved, and in fifteen minutes was dressed in grey flannels, a tweed coat, a scarf tied over an open-necked shirt. The morning's sun was dulling, and clouds were blowing up from the west; it would rain before midday, and it was now ten o'clock. He hurried along to the landing, and to the lift which led to the tower; and as far as he could make sure, no one saw him. He went up, reached the balcony landing and the blocked staircase, used the key and pressed the spot in a stone, which operated the revolving section of the wall. He had watched Rodney carefully and knew exactly how to do it.

As the door opened, radio music sounded, softly. He peered in. Hester was standing by the window and Mannering knew that she was staring down at Rodney. She had probably seen what happened outside.

Mannering said: "Hester."

She swung round, startled.

"Oh, I didn't hear you!"

"You ought to stand a chair here, anyone who comes is bound to shift it," he said. "Are you all right?"

"Yes, I—I'm fine."

"Is there anything you haven't told me?"

"No," answered Hester, very tensely. "But there's one thing I've only just realised, Mr. Mannering. Rodney really does hate his father, doesn't he? Do you—do you know why?"

CHAPTER FIFTEEN

PAST

"Yes," Mannering answered. "I know why."

Hester said: "Please tell me."

"Ten years ago, Lord Horton left his wife, Rodney's mother and there was a divorce. His wife was so distressed and worried by it that she took her own life."

He watched the girl closely as he related the bald facts, saw the concern and, gradually, the dawn of understanding in her clear eyes. She did not comment at once, so he went on:

"And Rodney has never forgiven his father."

"I suppose it's understandable," Hester said slowly. Mannering could sense the real relief she felt; at least there was a cause. "I knew that the present Lady Horton was his step-mother, but——" she broke off. "Why does Rodney stay here?

"He stays here when his step-mother is in London or abroad, but won't stay when she's here," Mannering answered. "One reason is that his father controls his money, and keeps a very tight hold on it. I've heard him threaten to walk out and emigrate, do anything but accept his father's hand-outs, but at other times he feels that the money is really his——"

"Is it?" interrupted Hester.

"It will be. Under his grandfather's will, the fortune goes from father to son. When he's twenty-five he gets some capital, but until then his father is his only source of income."

"I see." Hester looked fresher and younger, Mannering thought; she had slept soundly, probably she had been feeling much better until she had seen what happened outside. It was almost cruel to change her mood, but it had to be changed. "Hester, do you know any reason why Guy should be attacked?"

"Of course I don't," Hester answered. "I've been haunted about that all night. Is he—is he any better?"

"A little."

"Thank God for that! Mr. Mannering, I really must go to Mother."

"You can't, for a while," Mannering said. "Are you sure you know of no reason why anyone should attack Guy?"

"Absolutely none," Hester insisted. "I've never confided in him about Rodney or the blackmail. I told him I was desperately hard up, and wanted to borrow some money, but he didn't know why. When did it happen? Before or after Morgan——"

"After."

"Could he have seen who killed Morgan?" She was almost eager.

"Guy didn't see the murder," Mannering told her, and he found himself admiring the girl's quick grasp of the situation. "But he was near the gates about the time, the killer may have thought Guy saw him. Hester, is there anyone with a reason to want you dead, or out of the way?"

She didn't answer.

"Is there?" Mannering demanded.

"Well, yes," she answered. "If he knows about Rodney and me, Lord Horton would want me out of the way, wouldn't he? And I know that when Rodney had a love affair a year ago, his father did his best to drive the girl away."

She had the devasting logic of youth, and a mind as clear as crystal.

"Has anyone else got reason to want to harm you?"

"Of course not."

"Any jilted boy friend?"

"No," Hester answered flatly. "I've never had a

steady boy friend and there's no reason at all for anyone to want me out of the way, except Lord Horton."

And Horton had just had that vicious quarrel with his son.

Mannering was due to see his host at eleven o'clock, in the long gallery. He left Hester a little before eleven, after promising early news of her brother, and descended the spiral staircases slowly, waited for a few minutes by the lift, half expecting Rodney; but Rodney did not come. He went down in the lift, and then towards the long gallery, which ran the length of the great hall. It was from here that Horton Hall looked like a great mediaeval cathedral, and this the vast nave. Two stained glass windows, each sixteenth-century craftsmanship, were in the west wall. Great tapestries which would have graced the Vatican Museum or the palaces of France hung on these brick walls, which stood as sound and solid now as they had three or four centuries ago. Huge suits of armour, standing like mediaeval sentinels, were in the recesses made by each of the buttresses. Huge oaken furniture, shiny and almost black with an age of polish, loomed against the pale grey of the granite walls as if it would never be moved.

Here and there recesses in the wall were occupied by tiny figures; some carved, some cast, all bejewelled; and here was the great weakness of the Horton Collection; here was the place where the substitutions had first been made.

Horton was not here yet.

Mannering took advantage of the authority that allowed him to move two small pieces from their recesses to a single light which hung, oddly and incongruously, from a long flex; it was a jeweller's light. He did not stand at the small oak table where his tools and scales, calipers and record books were, but turned to the pieces, one an exquisite early English figure of a bishop, the other the figure of a young girl, draped with a jewelled cloak. The exquisite workmanship in itself was as rare as it was beautiful, and made each object precious; but the diamonds in the cloak which covered the girl from breast to waist should be real. Now, they scintillated and sparkled, but when Mannering took a small diamond brooch from a case and placed it at the same angle beneath the light, there was no doubt that it had greater brilliance than the figure; and the figure's diamonds should have been brighter. He cleaned the diamond cloak with a small brush wet with soapy water, then polished it with a leather; it sparkled a little more, but was still not as bright as it should have been. He turned it upside down, to see the markings on the base; there was little doubt that these were newer than they should have been.

This was a copy and these 'diamonds' were paste. It was worth perhaps a hundred pounds; and the value of the original was at least two thousand.

Mannering, used to working among beautiful and precious things, was suddenly and sharply disturbed by that fact: this one tiny object in his hand should be worth two thousand pounds, and when he glanced round there were a dozen, perhaps two dozen such objects, all of similar value. The wealth of the Hortons was fabulous; they were said to be one of the wealthiest families in Europe.

It was like being in a treasure house.

Mannering picked up the bishop, and almost immediately felt the curious attraction of real diamonds. It was an attraction he had known most of his life, a kind of magnetism. Even before he examined this, he believed that it was real. He derived a kind of excitement, divorced from all the circumstances of his investigation, from the murder and the blackmail, and from the feud between Lord Horton and his son.

Horton was late.

Mannering put the bishop down, and made an entry in the notebook he used as a record. Already he had examined over three hundred *objets d'art* and twenty or thirty of them were replicas. He had made a mental note of the total value of the missing items, and it was well over a hundred thousand pounds. This was crime in a grand manner.

He turned to put the two objects back in the recess, and then heard footsteps down below. They were heavy, and echoed through the great hall; only Horton walked like that and made so much noise. Mannering did not call, but watched as he came from the door leading into a courtyard and then into the park. From this height, sixty feet above the ground floor, the owner of the Hall and of this fabulous collection looked short and misshapen; almost as stocky as his son. He walked with deliberate tread towards a door beneath the gallery, and in a moment or two would be on his way up here; his footsteps would ring out clearly on the stone steps.

He disappeared.

Mannering had seen the scowl on his round face, knew that he was in an ugly mood, and was prepared for any kind of unpleasantness; what he had to decide was whether to let this pass, or whether to give Horton as good as he gave. The primary purpose in Mannering's mind was to find the truth about the murder; the rest would fit into place after that.

Horton's footsteps sounded again.

Then Mannering heard a different sound, soft and slithering; it was much nearer him. He swung round. A man with a scarf wound round his face and with a cloth cap pulled low over his head was by the desk, left hand outstretched for the record book, where Mannering made his notes on the quality of the pieces here— the real and the false; and his right hand pointing a gun at Mannering.

The man cried: "Don't move." He picked up the book and backed a pace, and the gun in his hand did not waver. Mannering's heart began to pound. The notes in that book were unimportant while he was alive—but if he were dead, then it was the only record of his findings.

Was this man going to kill him?

"Keep quiet," the man said sharply. The footsteps on the stairs seemed louder, and any moment the heavy door would open and Horton would stride into the gallery.

The man with the gun backed another pace; possibly he did not shoot because he had less chance to get away with someone else near.

Mannering called: "Barry! Don't come in!"

He saw the glint in the gunman's eyes, heard an exclamation from Horton, and prepared to throw himself forward. Then without warning, someone hooked his legs from under him. He crashed down, twisting his head round as he fell. He saw another man, face covered, bending over him, with his right hand raised; and in his right hand was a weapon of the kind which had been used in the attack on Guy Vane.

Mannering flung his hands up to try to save his head. He felt the blow, and took part of its weight on his left forearm, but the weapon struck his forehead too, and dazed him.

He heard a roar; from Horton.

Then he heard the unmistakable bark of a shot.

He was dizzy and helpless, his arms were folded over the back of his head, he was fearful of another blow. He heard a second shot, and tried to roll over, but could not. A man kicked him. Then he heard loud, echoing voices, and knew that servants were coming. He began to scramble to his feet, still dizzy, but able to stand upright. One of the men with a scarf was at the door. Horton lay in the doorway, his back to Mannering. The servants were in the hall and others were on the staircase. One man went rushing out, but the one who had attacked Mannering was still close.

Mannering took a long step towards him. He had to pull that scarf off, and take a good look at the face.

The man swung round.

Another shot echoed on the stairs.

Someone cried out, as if in pain.

Mannering snatched at the scarf, clutched it, and pulled it from the sharp-pointed face of a man he had never seen before. He saw the glitter in dark eyes and the set of thin lips.

Then the man rushed and struck at him savagely.

The weapon, a length of iron with a knobbed end, struck Mannering at the top of the right arm, and sent him staggering. The first blow and the effort he had just made had taken all his strength, and he came up against the low gallery wall and would have fallen but for its support. The face of the man in front of him seemed to be going round and round. There were two faces, three faces, and they were all close to him, all seemed to be mouthing at him. He gritted his teeth and tried to stand upright, but could not.

He felt the other's arm round his legs.

For a moment, he did not understand why. The faces had gone. All he could see were the shapes of the suits of armour, the furniture, the jewelled *objets d'art*, all merging into one another, and all seemed to be moving round and round in a whirlpool which went faster and faster. Then there came the grip at his legs.

Why?

He felt pressure against the back of his legs, and the stonework of the gallery wall pressed into the small of his back.

His feet left the ground.

Then he realised that the other was trying to topple him over; that in a moment he might be hurtling down to the stone floor below, to crash and to die.

The awfulness of the danger gave Mannering a

greater strength and clarity of vision. He spread his arms and clutched the stone balustrade, and tensed himself. The pressure against the small of his back was agonising, if it got worse his back would break. The pressure on his arms was great, too, and only the tips of his toes were touching the floor. But for the earlier blows he could have fought this man off, but now horror was close upon him. He could not last out much longer.

He felt a sharp pain on his knuckles; another, more agonising. He let go with his right hand. The pressure became worse, he felt himself actually balancing on the low wall, felt his head and shoulders toppling towards the floor; and to death.

CHAPTER SIXTEEN

PICTURE OF A MAN

MANNERING did not think he had a chance to escape.

Now that he was leaning backwards, his feet right off the ground, he saw only one thing clearly: a mental picture of the man who was sending him to his death. Every line on the sharp-featured face seemed to be thrown up in sharp relief; so did the glint in the brown eyes.

Mannering kicked out.

He felt his right shoe strike against something yielding, and for a moment the pressure eased. He was lying there, balanced on the foot-wide ledge, still gripping it with his left hand, and still with a chance. He dared not move swiftly. He began to edge himself forward, expecting every moment the other man to return to the attack.

Then he heard a shout, words which sounded like: "There's another," and a gasp: "Look!" He could see the vast nave-like ceiling, the great chandeliers, the massive oaken rafters. Then he heard a clatter of footsteps. Men gripped his legs, another leaned over the ledge and supported the back of his head and his shoulders. He was half lifted, half dragged, to the safety of the gallery. His back felt raw, as if it had been scraped over a saw, his head was bursting, and there was no strength left in him. He felt himself carried by two men, and laid on a great couch, and winced when his back was pushed against wood. He kept seeing that sharp-featured face—but now he could picture Horton's, too. There was a growing fear in him, that Horton had been killed. The attack had come so swiftly and suddenly, and there had been no time to do more than warn the man.

He felt a cold pad on his forehead, easing the burning pain. Men's voices sounded. He opened his eyes, and saw faces close to him, one man very close. Hands ran over his body, checking for broken bones. All he needed was a dressing on his back and a few hours' rest, then he would be himself.

He made himself say: "Is Lord Horton—badly hurt?"

"He'll be all right," answered the man who had examined his body. "Wounded in the arm, that's all. You'll be all right too, Mr. Mannering. I shouldn't talk too much now. Wait until you've had a cup of coffee and a couple of aspirins." He made it sound so casual. "How bad is your back?"

"It's—all right."

"I'd like to help you turn over, and have a look at it," the man said. "I'm a St. John Ambulance Brigade man, one of the Hall staff, sir, and I assure you that I won't do you any harm."

Mannering said: "Get me—to my room, will you?" He clenched his teeth against the pain at his back; if there was a serious injury, it would be there. He felt another surge of fear, in case he was more badly hurt than he realised.

"Just as soon as possible," the first-aid man assured him, and practically ignored Mannering's request. "What we're going to do is slide a blanket under you, and then turn you over on your face—don't worry about trying to turn round yourself, you'll be all right. Ready?"

The man would do whatever he wanted.

"Yes."

Mannering's back felt as if it would break as he was rolled over gently; could it really be worse? There was a kind of panic in him, and he hardly dared to breathe. Then he felt a gentle pressure upon the soreness, pressure which became more and more firm. He felt his shirt being pulled up, and after a moment the first-aid man said:

"I think it's just bruising, sir, I'll be surprised if it isn't. You won't be able to move about much for a few days, I'm afraid, but you should be all right after that. I think you'd be wise to stay here until the doctor comes and he confirms what I say, though."

"All right," Mannering muttered.

"I should stay on your stomach," the man went on. "Be more comfortable that way."

"Thanks. Are you sure about Lord Horton?"

"He's been able to walk downstairs, sir, just a flesh wound in the top of the arm."

"Were the men caught?"

"I'm afraid not, sir," another man answered; this was Simms. "One of the servants was badly wounded, and the man who tried to push you over actually climbed down one of the pillars." There was a note of admiration in the valet's voice. "The coffee will be along in a few minutes, sir."

The two men who had attacked Mannering were almost certainly the two who had so savagely attacked Guy Vane; probably the two who had killed Clive Morgan.

And now, he, Mannering, could recognise one of them.

How much danger did that spell?

The doctor came, pronounced Mannering's back badly bruised, and recommended cold compresses and very soft pillows; he said that it would be three or four days before Mannering could walk in comfort. Mannering wanted to call that nonsense, but by the time he had been helped to his room, his back was already stiff, and he felt as if he could walk only when he was bent almost double. At least his mind was much clearer. He wanted to know how the two men had gained entry to the hall, how they had discovered what he was doing, and how they had come to realise the significance of the record book. That had gone, of course. He had spoken to no one else about it; he could tell Horton just what had happened as soon as Horton came to see him. Meanwhile, he could remember most of the items he had checked; a day or so had been wasted, that was all.

There was another problem: how much to tell the police.

Mannering reclined in an easy-chair with billowy upholstery, half-dozing, his back feeling more tender than painful. He had taken tablets which the doctor had given him, and hot sweet coffee. It was a little after one o'clock. Because he was drowsy, some of the urgent matters did not press heavily on his mind.

He wanted to see Horton; and he wanted to see Rodney, about the girl.

Could she have been the murderess? Could she give a name to these men?

Could Guy describe them?

There were movements in the outer room, and a moment later Simms peered in.

"Hallo," Mannering greeted.

"You are awake, sir. Good." The valet smiled. "His lordship is coming in about five minutes."

"Fine," said Mannering. "Any more news?"

"I understand that the police are on the way, sir."

"Ah," said Mannering. "Well, come and help me sit up, will you?"

Sitting up was much more of an effort than he had hoped; he had to face the fact that he would be practically helpless for several days. True, he could have the *objets d'art* brought to him, but it would take much longer and be much less satisfactory.

Then Simms announced Horton.

Horton's left arm was in a sling, and the sleeve of his jacket hung loose. He looked pale and more flabby than usual but he walked briskly enough, stamping on his heels in exactly the same way as he had stamped across the floor of the great hall a few minutes before the attack. The door closed, and he sat on the arm of a chair and said:

"Damned sorry about this, John."

"Occupational risk," Mannering said. "I'm glad you weren't hurt too badly."

"Would have been, if you hadn't shouted," Horton said. "I'll always be grateful."

"Forget it."

"Not on your life." Horton's voice was strong enough, and he was uncannily like Rodney in some of the things he said and the attitudes he adopted. "Know what the swine came for?"

"My record book."

"They get it?"

"Yes."

"I wonder why they wanted it—they can't rub the details out of your memory, can they?"

"Only in one way," Mannering said.

"Tell me?"

"If I'd hit the floor of the hall head first I wouldn't have much memory left, and you would have had to put someone else on the job. They'd have had a few days' grace, anyhow."

"See what you mean," said Horton. "Think they were going to kill you?"

"Yes."

Horton growled: "It's a hell of a business, and I'm responsible because I brought you down here. Like to go back to London and forget all about it?"

Mannering grinned: "No."

"Didn't think you would," said Horton. "Well, I was warned not to bring you down here, as you know. Someone wants to make sure that we can't easily find out just how much stuff has been stolen and replaced with worthless replicas." He was probably the only man in the world who would have used the word 'stuff' to describe the priceless things in this great house. "I don't frighten easily but I don't care for this. You know my basic worry, don't you? How much has been stolen, and has Rodney taken all of it? Or is there someone else you don't know about?"

"That's it," Mannering said. "I'm a long way from sure, yet. What happened between you and Rodney this morning?"

Horton grimaced. "Did you see that?"

"Yes."

"You'll probably think that the major fault is mine, and you may be right," Horton said, in a hard voice. "The truth is that Rodney won't forgive and forget and there's nothing I can do about it. I asked him quite civilly if there was any truth in the story that he'd been seen in Winchester and Southampton with a girl, and I hoped he wasn't going to have another *affaire* with a tart."

"Why do you have to needle him?" Mannering asked.

"I'm damned if I know," Horton said, almost explosively. "The truth is that whenever I see him, I get edgy; and he does with me. We're the most unnatural father and son you can imagine. He hasn't confided in you about a girl, has he?"

"No."

Horton said: "This girl Vane—any idea where she is? I was told that Hennessy seems to think you have."

"The police have been wrong before," Mannering said dryly.

Horton looked at him intently, and then said: "I believe you could find her, and Hennessy probably thinks you could, too. Well I'm not going to quarrel about it. Anyone who killed Morgan and took the pressure off Rod did me a service, but—who employed Morgan? Who is employing these other men—Morgan certainly didn't work alone. Is there someone else who can start blackmailing Rodney? What else has the boy done? And it's worse because we know that someone is employing these other men. The ugly truth is that they were able to gain access to the Hall. That suggests someone on the staff might be involved. Or else Rodney is still under coercive pressure."

Mannering said: "Leave it at that, for the time being. What do you want to tell Hennessy?"

"That's one of the things I've come to see you about," admitted Horton. "Hennessy is nobody's fool, and he puts on an act that he can't behave as ruthlessly with the aristocracy as he can with a farm worker, but don't you believe it. What do you advise?"

"Tell him everything."

"Am I to take that literally?"

"Yes," said Mannering, and shifted his position gingerly. "I should tell him that you suspected that Rodney was taking real *objets d'art* and replacing them with replicas and that you thought he was being blackmailed, and you asked me to come and check how far this had gone, and how much was missing. You needn't prefer a charge. In fact there's a case for saying that some of the things are morally Rodney's, so this is a family quarrel and outside the law. If you tell Hennessy much less, he won't believe you."

"You may be right," Horton conceded. "How do we explain the loss of the record book and the attack on you?"

"We don't."

"But we tell Hennessy that Rodney is a suspect."

"If Rodney's behind it, he'll be caught eventually. If he isn't, being suspected won't do him any harm."

"I suppose not." Horton was silent for a long time, before he went on very stiffly: "All right, John. Have it your way. But you tell Hennessey. It's not the kind of statement I want to make to the police. I take it you'll see the whole thing through, as far as you can."

"Yes," Mannering assured him. "And as soon as I can."

Horton stood up. Mannering stared into that pale, flabby face, and the eyes which so often looked blank, despite their owner's sharp intelligence. Horton began to move away. Mannering let him get as far as the door, and then called:

"Barry."

Horton half turned. "Yes."

"How much does Rodney really mean to you?"

"You can judge for yourself, can't you?"

"Yes," agreed Mannering. "I can judge for myself. You'd rather get on terms with him again than anything else in your life, wouldn't you?"

"He's an obstinate young fool," Horton muttered, "but—oh, forget it!"

He turned and strode out.

Mannering watched, wondering what he would do when Hennessy knew, wondered whether Rodney had the faintest idea of the depth of his father's feeling. The visit had stimulated Mannering, but he was still confined to the easy-chair, and his back felt as if it were a mass of bruises. He knew that Simms would give him good warning of Hennessy's approach, and dozed again, wishing that he could have a full day and night's rest before he had to cope.

There was a tap at the door.

"Come in," Mannering called.

It was Simms, who did not usually tap, and who opened the door swiftly, and seemed to run forward. Behind him was the massive police inspector and at least one other man; there was also someone whom Mannering could not see properly: a woman.

Had the police searched, and found Hester?

If Hennessy came to attack now, he would find Mannering's resistance at its lowest.

Simms whispered: "Mrs. Vane's with the police, sir," and then added loudly: "Chief Inspector Hennessy, sir, by appointment."

Hennessy came in, and then Alicia Vane pushed past him and came swiftly to Mannering. He could see the great tension in her manner, the desperation in her eyes.

"I want to know where my daughter is," she said abruptly. "I'm quite sure you know."

CHAPTER SEVENTEEN

DISTRESS

ALICIA VANE was shocked when she saw Mannering.

She recalled him as looking tall, healthy, strong; and now she saw him lying back in an easy-chair that was half-couch, very pale, and with bruises on the side of his face, a swollen lip, and badly grazed hands. She realised, then, that Hennessy had used her as a tool; had not warned her that Mannering had been hurt, had simply told her what to ask, and that she should keep out of sight until the last moment. Now she stared at a man who was obviously sick, and the deep distress she felt worsened instead of eased.

Hennessy said: "What makes you so sure, Mrs. Vane?"

"He came back to my house after I'd left last night, and if he didn't come to tell my husband where Hester was, why should he come back?"

"Have you asked your husband?"

"Of course I have," Alicia said, so sharply that Hennessy actually recoiled. "I can't make him admit anything, but it's obvious that he knows." She turned back to Mannering, and there was pleading in her voice. "Mr. Mannering, if you know where she is, please tell me. I can't stand the uncertainty. The doctors say that it's still touch and go with Guy, in twenty-four hours I seem to have lost both of my children. If you can help, you must."

"If I can help, I will," Mannering promised, and his voice was stronger than she had expected. "I'm sorry about Guy, but at least he's in no further danger."

Hennessy said: "If you have any idea where to find Miss Vane, Mr. Mannering, you must tell us."

Mannering looked into Mrs. Vane's eyes.

She was puzzled by his expression, and read into it something which Michael had tried to give her, reassurance. He did not speak, and did not take any notice of Fred Hennessy or the detective with him; he was simply trying to give her a message, that she need not worry about Hester.

"If I were you I'd go home and get some rest," he said. "I promised you and your husband that I'd do everything that I can—and I will."

Hennessy showed a harsh, cruel streak.

"A man who can't look after himself isn't likely to be able to look after others, Mrs. Vane. Judge for yourself whether Mr. Mannering is capable of helping your daughter or anyone else for the time being."

Alicia didn't respond.

She felt quite sure that Mannering's words were intended to do exactly the same thing as his expression: go home and rest, he said in effect, and don't worry about Hester. All the anger and rage she had felt towards him had gone, just as her prejudice had faded last night. She felt that she could trust this man.

"Mr. Mannering——" Hennessy began.

Mannering said: "Inspector I've an urgent message for you that doesn't concern Miss Vane but which might be connected with the murder. And I've put off taking a dose of morphia so that I can talk to you before I go off to sleep."

Alicia realised that Hennessy had failed in what he had come to do. She did not know whether she had lost or won, but was easier in her mind when she left the room and the great house. She had told Hennessy, wildly, that she believed Mannering knew where Hester was; that had been when Hennessy had called to visit and question Michael that morning. Michael had been out in the market; the tomatoes and lettuce had to be picked and sorted, and she had made herself help.

Michael would be waiting when she got home.

A police car took her away from the great porch, and she looked round, to see the vast building outlined against the sky. There was no sun now, only grey skies, and the light gave the Hall a kind of sinister appearance which was almost frightening.

She wanted to get away.

Hennessy said sharply: "Well, what is this information?"

"I can ring the bell and persuade the doctor that I've got to have that injection now, and complete rest to follow it," Mannering reminded him, equally sharp.

"You don't seem to appreciate the seriousness of the position. This is a case of murder."

"Don't be a fool." Mannering knew his temper was dangerously near getting the better of him. "A would-be killer, one of the two I saw in the woods last night, nearly broke my back. It's more luck than anything else that I'm alive. That's how serious I know it is."

"If you insist on withholding information——"

"If I get any information I think will do you the slightest good, I'll give it to you," Mannering said. "For instance—that Rodney Horton has been taking precious articles from this house and replacing them with replicas. That he was being blackmailed because of it. That Lord Horton sent for me to make a valuation to find out how much was missing."

Hennessy looked bewildered for a moment, and then snapped his fingers at the big sergeant, who took out a notebook and began to write, his eyes flickering from his notes to Mannering. The telling took no more than three minutes; at the end of them, Hennessy knew everything except the fact that much more than Rodney admitted taking was missing.

Mannering felt very tired when he finished.

"Very grateful, Mr. Mannering," Hennessy said, more mildly. "You won't regret giving us this information, I assure you. Now, this man you actually saw. Will you describe him please? We're coming to the gallery for finger-prints and we actually found the scarf you pulled from the man's face. With a bit of luck, we'll soon get him."

Mannering gave a full description, but found it difficult to concentrate; the effort of talking to Hennessy had taken a lot out of him. Hennessy went off in one of his mild moods, and soon afterwards Horton's doctor came in. He was a short, bald, rotund and jocund man, with plump, very white hands. He fiddled with a hypodermic syringe as if he enjoyed it, and Mannering watched him pierce the tiny bottle so as to fill the syringe.

"This'll put you off in a few jiffs," he said. "Ready?"

"Fire."

"Nice to know you've a sense of humour," the doctor said, and jabbed. "This'll keep you quiet for twelve hours or more, and when you come round you'll feel a new man. The X-ray shows that your back's only badly bruised. The danger might be a slipped disc later, but we'll look after that when the time comes. Your wife's coming up this evening. I told her that there was no great hurry."

"Thanks," Mannering said. "Everything may be solved by the time I come round."

"Could be, but it isn't likely," said the doctor, and rinsed his syringe in a glass of water. He seemed to relish filling and emptying it. "That's quick-working stuff I've given you—don't be surprised if you begin to feel drowsy almost at once."

"I'm drowsy," Mannering said, and meant it. He could feel the effect of the drug sweeping over him, and already there was much greater comfort in his back. In a few minutes he would be asleep, and the odd thing was that he did not mind; in twelve hours he could tackle anything that was thrown at him, but now—

"Has young Rodney been questioned, do you know?" he asked, and thought vaguely of Hester up in her eyrie.

The doctor was putting the syringe away.

"Eh?"

"Has Rodney been questioned?"

"Be difficult," the doctor answered, and closed a drawer in his case and grasped it.

"Why difficult?"

"My dear chap, you can worry about this when you've had some rest."

Mannering said sharply: "Don't play the fool." His head was swimming, his limbs were feeling numb, he knew that in a few minutes if not in a few seconds he would be under the influence of the drug. "Why——"

"Rodney's gone to London," the doctor said. "He caught the first train after lunch."

Mannering stared at him.

In his mind's eye he saw Hester, up in that Tower Room, watching from the window, living minute to minute for Rodney to come and see her; to take her food; to take her news. Why had he gone to London? How long would he be? Mannering tried to sit up, but could not. The doctor came towards him and said something which Mannering did not catch; he felt the pressure of the man's fingers on his arm, and felt the waves of unconsciousness coming over him. He tried to mouth the words: "Tower Room, Tower Room. Key's there." But he did not know whether he made himself understood or not.

The doctor said to Simms: "Do you know why Mr. Mannering should have been alarmed because Mr. Rodney has gone to London?"

"No, doctor, I've no idea."

"It's odd. He tried to say something, but couldn't get

it out," went on the doctor. "Probably nothing like so important as he thought it was. There's no need to watch him, but you'd better look in after four or five hours."

"Very good, sir," said Simms.

Hester stood by the window of the tower room, seeing the drive and watching the spot where Rodney and his father had met that morning. It was hours ago, and she seemed to think that if she stared at that spot long enough, she would be able to will Rodney to come and tell her what had happened.

Suddenly, she saw a familiar car: Hennessy's. It seemed to be coming away from the Hall, but there was a circular drive and two approaches, and it was possible that he was coming here to look for her. She saw Lord Horton appear, on foot, and Hennessy's car stopped. Hennessy got out, and she watched the two men as they spoke. They were remarkably alike in size and build. Hennessy glanced round towards the Hall, and for a moment she thought that he was looking straight at her; but he showed no sign, and Horton did not look up at the tower.

Then Hennessy got back into his car and drove off, and Lord Horton walked towards the Hall and disappeared from sight. The beautiful grounds were empty in the afternoon sunlight. She kept watching the drive in the hope that Rodney was on his way, but no one came.

She was getting hungry.

Rodney had brought a snack for her lunch, and she had eaten that nearly two hours ago. Because of the excitement and the comings and goings at the Hall, she had forgotten that she had eaten so little. Now it was after five o'clock.

Why hadn't Rodney come?

Hester left the window, and went to the door. She knew that it could be opened and he had promised to show her how and where; when he had come up that morning he had been in too much of a hurry, and now she began to wonder what he had had on his mind.

There was one good thing: if Rodney didn't come, Mannering would.

She switched on the radio, but it was Children's Hour on the Home Service and a talk on the Light. She went to a record-player and put on some records, but was in no mood for light music.

She hated the loneliness and was more and more worried about Guy.

In a way it would have been better to have faced the police than be stranded here. She would feel better as soon as one of the men came, but now she could not think about anything but the fact that she was getting more and more hungry and was scared.

It was dusk.
No one had come.
She was frightened, now.
Then she saw a taxi coming up the drive, and prayed that it meant help.

CHAPTER EIGHTEEN

LORNA MANNERING

LORNA MANNERING saw the great mass of the Hall as her taxi left the trees and came into the open parkland. In the dusk, the building seemed enormous. She could see light at some of the windows, but no one was about. Then the taxi stopped, and immediately two men came from the great front door.

One was Simms, whom she knew slightly.

"Good evening, Simms. How is my husband?"

"He's sleeping as sound as you could wish, ma'am," Simms assured her, and helped her out. The other man was already paying the taxi. "We are extremely sorry that we could not have a car at the station, it's been a very difficult day."

"That's all right," Lorna said.

As she stepped into the great hall, and the vastness lit only by electric replicas of old oil torches fastened in the walls, she felt the overpowering immensity of it. She knew what had happened, and saw the gallery wall from which John had nearly fallen. In this light, it looked deadly. She walked briskly a little ahead of Simms, a woman of more than average height, wearing a dark green suit, a small green hat on dark, wavy hair; the light was especially kind to her, and there was no doubt of her beauty. But just now, as often when in repose, she seemed to be frowning and almost sullen. In fact, she was anxious and worried.

A heavily built man who was probably a plain-clothes detective was working in the gallery; she saw him when she walked up the great staircase. Then Simms led her along familiar passages towards the suite where Mannering lay; they had visited the Hall several times, and were always housed in the same rooms. She caught her breath as she went into the bedroom, and saw John lying on his side, very pale, and so still that he might almost be dead. She fought down a moment of panic, and watched, making sure that he was breathing; there was only the slightest of movement at his lips.

She turned away.

"Dr. Richards said that he would look in again tonight," Simms told her, "and he said that it would probably be a week before Mr. Mannering could get about freely again—and even then he would have to be very careful."

"Yes," Lorna said. She did not want to talk to the valet too much; Horton would tell her what had happened, and she did not want to hear the same story twice. "Did Mr. Mannering leave any message for me?"

"No ma'am, but——" Simms hesitated. "There was a message from Mr. Rodney, just before he left. He said that he had to go to London for several days, and asked Mr. Mannering to look after everything."

"Do you know what he meant?" asked Lorna.

"I'm afraid not, ma'am," Simms said. "He did start to say something else, but didn't finish."

"What was it?" Lorna asked.

"He said that he was sure Mr. Mannering would look after 'her' but he didn't say whom he meant," Simms answered. "There is just a possibility that he was referring to the young lady who is wanted by the police for questioning about the murder of Clive Morgan."

"You mean, Hester Vane?"

"That's right, ma'am," Simms said. "Mr. Hennessy —one of the Gilston detective force—seemed to think that Mr. Mannering might know where she was."

"Do you know?"

"I've no idea at all," Simms assured her. "I do

know that Mr. Mannering was hoping to go and see Mr. and Mrs. Vane this evening. And he tried to give the doctor a message of some kind, which worried him, before he became unconscious. That's all I can tell you, I'm afraid."

"Thank you. How about the boy, Guy?"

"I believe he's still very ill," Simms answered.

"I see," said Lorna. She took off her hat and poked her fingers through her hair. "Where is Lord Horton?"

"He regretted that he had been called away, and said that he would be here by eight o'clock at the latest," Simms told her. "He asked that you should not wait dinner, ma'am."

"I'll wait, until half-past eight," Lorna said. "Thank you, Simms."

Simms bowed and went out.

Lorna looked even more sombre when the door closed, and she went back to look at John. Was it imagination or was he frowning? The story of his anxiety to give the doctor a message might make her think that; in fact, there were lines at his forehead and the corners of his mouth which suggested that even subconsciously, he was worried. She turned away and went into the dressing-room. Her case had been brought up; she had packed only enough for the night or two, but it was the custom to change at the Hall, and she had brought a cocktail dress. She went into the bathroom and had a shower, trying to think of anything she could do.

Why had he been so worried?

Was there any connection between that and this missing girl?

She had talked to John on the telephone, and he had told her some, but not all of the details; he was habitually inclined to keep things from her, in case she worried.

This was a peculiar affair in every way. All the key people seemed to be missing. If she knew why young

Rodney had gone to London, it might help; and if she could judge why Horton himself had left the Hall and would be back late, that would ease things. As it was, she felt as if she had been pitched into the middle of a puzzle without having a single clue.

Dr. Richards arrived just before eight o'clock, very apologetic because he was late. He felt John's pulse, examined his eyes, hummed and hahed, said that it looked as if John would be one to take the drug severely; he would probably not come round until the morning.

In the tower room, Hester was standing by the tiny window. She had not pulled the shutters, and the light was shining out; but she did not know whether anyone would notice it, and there was no way in which she could attract attention.

She was desperately hungry; and solitude was turning fear to terror.

It was nearly nine o'clock when Lorna called Simms, and said that she would have dinner in her room if Lord Horton wasn't back. Simms assured her that his lordship was not. The meal was beautifully cooked and served, but she had little appetite. She felt oppressed by the frown still on John's face, by the possibility that there were deep causes for fear. A little after half-past nine, she left the room and went towards the great gallery, because that was where John had been attacked. She approached it from one side, and saw the great drop to the stone floor and realised how lucky he was to be alive.

She knew that he loved not only this place but the beauty of the Horton Collection.

She looked across, and saw two men, standing by one of the recesses. She saw the lighting inside it, a glow which was there to set off the precious pieces inside. One man was handling an object, as if with great caution. There was something almost furtive about the way they were standing close together and talking in low-pitched voices. No one else was near. She glanced downstairs, and saw no sign of the big man she had taken for a plainclothes man.

She looked round, and saw that there were the hanging cords of bells at several places, she would always be within reach of an alarm. On tip-toe, so as not to make a noise with her heels, she went along the gallery, keeping in the shadows cast by the great chandeliers. She knew that she was passing a fortune, but she thought of nothing but the two men.

The man who had handled the piece was putting it back. She saw his profile, sharp against the light, and was surprised into a whispered exclamation.

"That's Largent."

Anthony Largent was one of the most reputable dealers in London. He was in the same field as John, and the two men often did business together, although they had never been close friends. Largent had a hooked nose and a small pointed beard; he always gave the impression that he was posing.

He moved to another recess, and the light at this was switched on; all the lights in the great hall and the gallery were seldom on at one time; only on great occasions. She saw the glass panel in front of the *objet d'art* pushed to one side. With every step Lorna was drawing nearer, and now she could hear the sounds they were making. Suddenly, the bigger of the two men moved into her line of vision, and she recognised Horton.

Had he deliberately avoided her?

In any case, why should he deal first with John and then with Largent? He knew perfectly well that they were competitors. To have one here while the other was lying helpless because he was trying to help was unbelievably cynical.

Lorna saw the *objet d'art* that they were handling, saw

the jewels glitter, and knew that it was the figurine of a girl wearing a jewelled cloak.

She heard Horton say:

"What about this one?"

Largent was examining it closely, and it was a long time before he answered:

"It is genuine."

"Are you sure?"

"My dear sir, I am positive." There was a haughty tone in the dealer's voice.

Horton said: "Mannering told me that it was a replica."

"I don't care who told you differently, Horton. This is one of the two figurines made for the court of Louis XIV as a birthday present for Queen Maria Theresa. The other is in the Louvre. This one is in Horton Hall."

Horton didn't speak.

"What else do you wish me to examine?" asked Largent.

"I want you to go through everything here just as soon as you can," Horton said. "How long will it take you?"

"Three days," Largent told him, without hesitating.

"That will be soon enough," said Horton, 'Mannering won't be about in less than three days." He took the figurine from Largent's hands, replaced it, pushed the sliding glass window into position, and then locked it at one side. "Now we had better go to my study, Mrs. Mannering may come out of the dining-room I don't want her to see us here."

"Will she expect to see me here to-morrow?" asked the other man.

"Tomorrow will be all right, I shall tell her that I had to have expert opinion quickly. I wanted to make sure about these pieces. I find it hard to believe that Mannering would mislead me, but——"

"This figurine and all the other pieces I have seen

are genuine," Largent repeated haughtily. "Mannering may have been mistaken. He would hardly give you a wrong opinion deliberately."

There was a long pause, before Horton said:

"Wouldn't he?"

Lorna stayed in the shadows of a tall chest, and waited for the two men to go. They made little sound on the gallery itself, but once they were on the staircase, they walked quite normally. She stayed until they appeared in the hall. From here she could see that Horton's arm was still in a sling. He looked twice as broad and big as Largent, who was tall and willowy. They disappeared into one of the passages which led to the West Wing—the dining-room and the living quarters.

She felt fiercely angry; and quite helpless.

John would never have made a mistake about that figurine; nothing would ever make him commit himself to an opinion unless he was positive. Either Largent had lied to Horton—or the genuine *objet* had been put there in place of the replica.

She did not know how to make sure which.

It was like a conspiracy, against John.

Mannering lay in his room, drugged.

Hester was sitting in one of the large easy chairs, staring at a silent radio. She was past ordinary hunger, now, and was getting into a great state of terror. The water had been turned off, and there was very little left in the one jug which Rodney had filled for her; and there was no food of any kind.

It was nearly midnight.

She could just see the stars through the small window, but toughened glass had been fitted in the days when this had been the strong-room. She could not break it, in order to throw out a note, or to throw out anything to attract attention. Now and again she would jump up in desperation and go to the window and pound against it; and she would pound on the door. But neither the window nor the door budged.

She hated the silence.

Strangely, it was a little less terrifying now, because she felt more drowsy than hungry and thirsty. Her head ached. She wanted to sleep, prayed that she would drop off, and that Rodney or Mannering would come to her while she slept.

It was a long time since she had jumped up from that chair.

CHAPTER NINETEEN

OLIVE BRANCH

ALICIA VANE saw the car draw up outside the front of the bungalow, and knew at once that it was Hennessy's. In the past few days she had almost forgotten that he had been a family friend, had almost forgotten the fact that he and Michael had known each other for many years. She had just come from the hospital, and there was no change in Guy's condition, so this could have nothing to do with that.

She saw Hennessy get out of the car, approach hesitatingly, and then move quickly, obviously because he saw Michael near the office shed. Hennessy disappeared. Alicia did not want to talk to him, but was anxious to know what he had to say.

She went out into the kitchen.

She saw Hennessy and Michael shake hands, and could have slapped Michael. Yet she could not mistake the look of relief on Hennessy's face.

The window was open. She stood to one side, so that neither of the others could see her if they glanced round.

"Well, Ted," Michael said. "What news have you got for us?"

"Nothing good, I'm afraid," answered Hennessy. "I haven't come officially, Mike."

"Oh."

"I know it's going to be difficult to make you realise it, let alone Alicia, but I've had to do what I've done."

"I know," Michael said, but at least he didn't thaw too much and too quickly. "Mind if I'm frank?"

"I want you to be."

They were like two boys, Alicia thought.

"You've been bloody ham-handed about the whole

thing," Michael said, and Alicia was surprised into a quick approving smile.

"It's been damned difficult," Hennessy argued. "The trouble is, Mike, that the evidence against Hester is so strong. The fact that Guy was attacked and these fellows attacked Mannering as well doesn't really alter that, you know. Hester could be involved. You and Alicia know she's been behaving oddly lately. We've assumed that it was blackmail, but supposing it's something else? And for God's sake don't tell me that you know your daughter too well to think that she would lie to you. She'd lie, like we all would, if we were in a tight corner."

And Hester had lied about some things, Alicia reminded herself.

"Well, where do we go from here?" Michael asked. "If you really think Hester's guilty——"

"I didn't say that, I said the evidence is all against her," Hennessy put in hurriedly. "And the longer she's in hiding the worse it will look. I've just come from the Chief Constable. He's told me that unless we see the end of it by tomorrow, he'll call in the Yard. I've spent hours today with him and with the Chief Superintendent, and we've been through all the evidence with a fine-toothed comb. We don't know for sure whether Hester killed Morgan, but we do know she was near the car when he was killed. At the least she may have something which would help us find the murderers. You and Alicia may not agree, but the best way Hester can help herself is to give herself up."

Alicia went to the door, opened it, and stepped outside. Michael swung round; Hennessy was already facing the door, and Alicia saw the way his lips tightened and realised how much he expected her to oppose him.

But at least she now knew that it was useless to blame Hennessy for anything.

"It's all very well to say that, Ted," she said, and saw

his face light up at her tone. "But how do we know that you're right? You haven't been very clever yet, have you? I don't mean that nastily, but Mr. Mannering told you about the two men who attacked Guy, and they're still free."

"If we knew all the facts, if we could question Hester for instance, we would probably be able to get results quicker," Hennessy said eagerly.

"I can see his point of view," Michael conceded.

"I'm not interested in a point of view, I'm just interested in making sure that Hester's safe," Alicia declared. "Anyhow, we don't know where Hester is."

"Mannering does," Hennessy put in quickly. "He's out of action and won't be any use to Hester or anyone for a week or more. Why don't you make him tell you where she is? If you keep at him, he'll tell you. And I tell you that if we don't find Hester soon, the situation will be even worse."

Neither Alicia nor Michael answered.

Hennessy said flatly: "You've got to make up your minds whom to trust—a stranger like Mannering, or me and the police. Good God! You don't think I *want* to do Hester any harm, do you? It would be like harming my own daughter!"

Alicia could feel the sincerity which glowed in him.

"I'll take it up with Mannering as soon as he's able to see me," Michael promised, and Alicia did not argue, for she now knew that it was the only wise thing to do. "Do you know when he'll be able to talk?"

"I'll check," Hennessy promised, still eagerly. "He may be round tonight. If not, first thing in the morning. May I use your telephone?"

"Ten o'clock in the morning is the first chance we'll get," Hennessy told them when he had spoken to the Hall. "I talked to Mrs. Mannering."

Lorna turned away from the telephone in the sitting-room of the suite, and went to the bedroom, to see John lying motionless. At times, his stillness and his pallor frightened her. There was no hint of colour in his cheeks, but there seemed to be dark shadows at his eyes. She closed the door and went back to the dressing-room's fireside. Simms had built a log fire, but it was not really cold. She stared into the flames, and kept hearing those whispered voices, and Horton and Largent's final conclusion: that John had been mistaken about some of the pieces he had said were replicas. She was more than ever sure that Largent was wrong, but until she could talk to John, there was no way of proving it. If he didn't recover consciousness in the morning——

She had told Vane that he could come at ten o'clock. Now she wondered whether that would be late enough. She was restless and worried—not only about John but about Hester Vane. The more she heard about the circumstances the more sure she felt that John had hidden her somewhere for good reasons of his own. The why didn't matter; the hiding place did.

She had not yet seen Horton, and when Simms came in she wasn't surprised that he told her:

"His lordship is home, ma'am, and asks whether you would like him to come and see you, or whether you would care to join him in the study."

"I'll join him," Lorna said. "Tell him I'll be along in five minutes."

"Very good, ma'am."

Lorna looked hard at Simms as he went out. There was something about the man that she didn't like, but she could not put a name to it; it was almost as if he was watching her. It would hardly be surprising if he reported everything she did and said to Horton.

She walked along the gallery towards the staircase, and was acutely aware of the fact that the two men had been there. She went down the wide staircase towards the main hall and then rounded them and went to the room where John had seen Guy: she had been told about Guy's visit. John had helped Hester, and she had vanished; had promised to help Guy, and he had been savagely attacked; had said that he would help Rodney, and Rodney had disappeared.

It was almost as if this were a campaign against John.

Nonsense?

She went into the study. Horton was on his own, sitting near a bigger, warmer fire than the one upstairs. He jumped up at sight of her, and approached with his good hand outstretched. She distrusted him far more than she distrusted Simms, in spite of Horton's smile, his heartiness, and the powerful grip of his left hand.

"Lorna, my dear, how good to see you." He held her hand a moment too long. "I'm dreadfully sorry about all this, and it's worse because I had to be out when you came. How is John?"

"He's still unconscious," Lorna answered.

"Richards told me that he might be out for twenty-four hours or more," Horton remarked. "It will do him good, too. Pity he is going to be *hors de combat* for a bit, but it can't be helped. Sit down, and tell me all about yourself. Whose pictures have you been painting lately?" He was talking too much and too rapidly, to cover a guilty conscience, of course; he did not intend to tell her about Largent yet. "One of these days I would like you to paint Rodney's, it's time he had a portrait done. Now, what is it to be? Brandy? Liqueur?"

"May I just have coffee?"

"My dear, of course." Horton pulled a long rope, the bell-pull. "Do sit down. I——"

He glanced round as the telephone bell gave a sharp ring, and stopped. He didn't move towards it, but

Lorna had the impression that he was expecting a call that he did not much like.

It rang again.

"Sorry," he said. "If the maid comes in while I'm talking, order what you want, will you?" He lifted the telephone and glanced at Lorna, and she had a strong feeling that he wished that she were not here. "Lord Horton speaking," he announced, and waited.

The door opened, and a small, thin woman came in.

Horton exclaimed: "*What?*" and seemed to recoil from the telephone. The woman stopped in her tracks. Lorna turned round to Horton, and all other thoughts were driven from her mind. He looked dreadful, all the heartiness had vanished.

There was a long pause.

"How—how badly?" he asked, and Lorna stood up, approaching him; he looked as if he might fall.

"I see. Very well. I'll come at once."

He replaced the receiver slowly, and for the next few moments everything he did was very deliberate, as if he was suffering from a severe shock. He saw Lorna and saw the maid, moistened his lips as if he was about to speak, but said nothing.

Lorna made herself ask: "What is it, Barry?"

He closed his eyes; and it was a fact that he looked older, and somehow shrunken.

"Rodney," He said. "The police in London—want to question him. They—they had a warrant for his arrest, for—for dealing in stolen jewels. He——"

Horton couldn't finish.

Peters drew in a hissing breath.

Lorna found herself touching Horton's sound arm, as if that would give him a little strength.

"He tried to get away, and ran into a car," Horton said, in that same shocked voice. "He was badly injured, and is in Westminster Hospital. I—I must go." He squared his shoulders, and became more brisk.

"Peters, tell Black to bring the Rolls-Royce round at once. Have some things packed and send Morrison after me with them—take them to the Arturo Club, and telephone them to say that I will probably arrive about one o'clock."

"Very good, sir," the maid said, and withdrew.

Horton looked at Lorna. She saw the pain in his pale grey eyes, and realised what John had realised earlier in the day; there was deep love in him for his only son. He moistened his lips again, as if he wanted to say something but could not find the words. Then he spoke in a hard voice:

"I'm sorry about this. Lorna, there's something you must know. John must, too. I had to find out quickly how much Rodney had taken away from here. When the doctor told me that John could not hope to be about for several days, I sent for Largent. He's staying in Gilston, but he will be out here in the morning. I meant to tell you then, but felt embarrassed as John was ill. You must forgive me, but—but if that boy was so frightened that he resisted arrest and ran away from the police, then he must have committed a black crime indeed, a black crime."

He seemed to be muttering to himself.

Lorna said: "Of course you had to send for Largent, John will know that. I hope Rodney——"

Words were so little use.

"If he dies——" Horton said, then broke off, bit his lips, and moved suddenly towards the door. She watched him go. She knew that within five minutes he would be going down the drive; that in a little more than two hours he would be at his son's bedside. Horton's son—and Vane's son. It was a strange parallel.

There was still a great deal that she did not understand, but she told herself that if Rodney died, it would be a paralysing blow to his father.

If Rodney died. . . .

Up in the tower room, Hester was lying curled up on an easy-chair, with a rug over her. It was chilly; not really cold, but cold enough to promise real cold during the night. She was only vaguely aware of it as she sat there, curled up for warmth, feeling almost as if she were doped.

CHAPTER TWENTY

MANNERING WAKES

When Mannering first came round, he did not know where he was, and was semi-conscious for a few minutes. It was dark. He was not aware of Lorna, asleep in the bed next to him, but could hear the ticking of a clock. He had no conscious thought, just an awareness of trouble and anxiety; but he felt himself going under to the waves of sleep again, and succumbed.

When he next came round, it was light; and he knew that the light came from the window. He stared at it. There was exceptional brightness, as if the sun were striking the glass, and he felt very warm. He was still aware of a sense of anxiety, but did not at first realise what it was about. Then he heard someone call out, in the grounds, and although he did not recognise the voice, he was immediately reminded of Hester.

He started.

His back seemed to be slashed with pain.

He lay quite still, reminded so viciously of what had happened, and knowing that he could not move with any comfort, and sudden movement would be agonising. Even then, he was sweating from the slash of pain. He lay very still, while all the thoughts poured through his mind, and he recalled everything.

He turned his head.

He saw Lorna's comb and brushes on the dressing-table; Lorna's handbag; a handkerchief; other oddments which told him that she was at the Hall. That was the first moment of relief. He turned his head cautiously, as if that might hurt, and looked at the closed door. It was possible that she was in the other room. He opened his mouth to speak, hesitated, and then called:

"Lorna."

His voice sounded weak, and he doubted whether it would reach the ears of anyone in the outer room. He sweated still more. He lay without moving, aware of tenderness more than soreness now, and worried about his back; that pain had not been normal. But he was still in the Hall, and if there were anything really serious, he would have been taken to hospital; with Guy Vane.

"*Lorna!*"

There was no answer.

He wondered what time it was; somewhere about eleven o'clock in the morning, judging from the sun. And he wondered what day it was. It seemed a long time since he had been attacked and it would not surprise him to learn that he had been unconscious for forty-eight hours; but against that he reminded himself that if he had been so seriously injured, he would have been in a hospital.

Unless they dared not move him.

"*Lorna!*" he called.

There was still no answer.

He could stretch out and touch the bell at the side of the bed; it might be painful to move like that, but he could do it. That would bring Simms, and he preferred to talk to Lorna, to let her know first that he was conscious. The first question to ask was about Hester Vane. He was edgy about Hester, but told himself that there was no need to be, for Rodney would surely have come back by now, and released her.

Then he saw a newspaper.

It lay on a small table, near the bed but not alongside it. At first, he looked at it with only idle curiosity, for it did not seem important. Lorna did. He deliberated whether to wait for her, hoping that when she came back to the suite the first thing she would do was to look in at him, or whether to touch that bell.

Then he read the headline, which was upside down to him and looked peculiar. Double e's always did when seen upside down. PEER'S SON INJURED, he spelt out, and then drew in a sharp breath, as he thought of Rodney. Peer's son what? It might mean anything. Could this be about Rodney, and if it were, what had he done to hit the newspaper headlines?

Mannering had to get that newspaper, but it was out of reach unless he stretched from the bed. He edged over, cautiously. His back was very tender and painful, but the agonising streak of pain did not come. The newspaper was within a foot of his outstretched hand, and he was as close to the edge of the bed as he could get. Now he could only hope to reach it by rolling over; if he should fall, he would not be able to get up by himself. Nothing else would have persuaded him but those words seemed to shout at him. PEER'S SON IN——
He began to edge himself over to his side. Once on his side he could roll over on to his stomach. Pain stabbed through his back, and he winced and relaxed. He must ring the bell.

He could just touch it.

He felt furious with himself because he was so helpless, but there was no real cause for reproach. He lay back, sweating, worrying. It seemed a long time before any sound came, and he began to wonder whether the bell had been heard. Usually Simms came very quickly, he had a small room just across the passage and was generally there. Mannering, clenching his teeth, was about to press the bell again when the door opened.

Lorna came in.

"John!" She paused on the threshold, then hurried across to him. "Darling, what have you been doing? You're half out of bed."

"Sorry," he managed to say, and looked into her face, eagerly. She kissed him. The pressure of her body against his for a moment hurt his back. She drew away. "What were you trying to do?" she demanded. "If you make your back any worse you'll be laid up for months."

"I wanted—the newspaper." Mannering felt very weak, and was sweating; his forehead was clammy.

She glanced at it.

"Oh," she said, and went across and picked it up. "Darling, there isn't a thing you can do."

"Is it—Rodney?"

"Yes."

"Not—not one of my good cases," Mannering said, and gave a twisted smile. "I'm on my back, and—never mind. What—does it say?"

Lorna held out the front page of the *Daily Globe* so that he could read it, and immediately he drew in a sharp breath; and he realised that Lorna could see the alarm in his eyes. For the headlines read:

PEER'S SON INJURED WHILE RESISTING ARREST

"How—badly?"

"Very badly."

"When?"

"Last night, in London."

"Last night—darling, how long have I been here?"

"Fifteen hours, the doctor tells me," Lorna said. "John, what's worrying you?"

"And Rodney hasn't come back?"

"No."

"God," Mannering groaned, and closed his eyes. "Lorna——"

"John, whatever it is, there isn't a thing you can do about it, and I'm not going to let you try to do anything," Lorna said. He knew the tone of old: the tone almost of desperation, because she knew that if he was really set on some course of action, there was nothing she could do to prevent him from taking it.

She wouldn't try to prevent anything he wanted to do now. He felt a tension greater than he had known it since he had come to the Hall, and the tension passed itself on to her. She stood close to the bed, and he stared up into her eyes, and said:

"Has Hester Vane been found?"

"No."

"She——"

"Darling," Lorna said, and rested a hand on his shoulder. "The girl has to look after herself. It's obvious that she's been lying, and that she got herself into this trouble. She must get herself out of it."

That sidetracked Mannering.

"Who said she'd been lying?"

"All the evidence——"

"It often lies itself."

"John, Superintendent Morrison's here, from the Yard. I've just been talking to him, and the evidence against Hester is greater than ever it was. The knife that was used to kill Morgan was her brother's. She'd borrowed it the day before the murder—one of the assistants at her shop told the police that."

Mannering said: "Positive?"

"It was found late last night in the woods near the gates, and her parents admitted that she had borrowed it—she often did, apparently, for getting stones out of the tyres of her motor-scooter. Don't even think of trying to do anything more for her, John. Tell the police where she is, and be done with it."

"Lorna——"

"It's no use arguing!"

"She's in the tower suite here. She must have been there for nearly twenty-four hours without food."

"No!" Lorna was badly shaken by that. "But——"

"No one uses it these days. Rodney has one key. I've got the other."

Mannering broke off.

Unthinking, he had moved, and the pain stabbed again, he had to clench his teeth against it. Lorna's alarm was at least reassuring.

"It's in my trousers pocket," Mannering said, and Lorna jumped up and went to the wardrobe. "I want to talk to her before anyone else sees her."

"John, you're not fit to——"

"I don't talk with my back!"

"You talk out of the back of your neck sometimes," Lorna said, and began to rummage through the pockets of his trousers, which were on a hanger.

"Simms may have emptied the pockets," Mannering said. And of course, Simms would, it wasn't possible to think normally about the ordinary things. "Is my loose change on the dressing-table?"

Lorna looked.

"No," she said, and glanced to the mantelpiece, then at a small chest. "There it is," she added, and stepped across the room. Even now, Mannering saw the easy grace with which she moved, and felt that tension in her manner. "There's your key case."

"This key's loose," Mannering said. "A long, thin one."

She looked at the pile of silver and coppers, at a wallet, handkerchief, leather key case, all the oddments which the valet had taken out, but she didn't speak.

"Darling, hurry," Mannering urged.

Lorna looked round.

"There's no other key here."

"There must be. It's a long one, with a complicated-looking barrel."

"There's no other key here," Lorna insisted, picking up the key case and opening it. Mannering watched her with great intensity, until she said: "It isn't here, either."

"It must be!"

"John, don't keep saying 'it must be'. It isn't, and that's all there is about it. Are you sure that you had it?"

"Of course I'm sure," Mannering said. "Simms——"

He stopped.

He had rung the bell for Simms at least ten minutes ago, but there had been no response.

"Where's Simms?" he asked sharply.

"I haven't seen him this morning," Lorna answered. "John, where is this tower suite?"

"It's the old gallery, blocked off at the upper spiral staircase in the days when it was a kind of museum. There were just two keys. Rodney took them, and used the place to sulk in. That girl's been there without food——" Mannering broke off. "You'd better call for the police right away."

"Another half-hour or so won't make any difference to her," Lorna said. "Her mother and father are coming to see you at twelve o'clock—that's in twenty minutes' time. They were coming earlier, but I put them off. Hadn't you better talk to them first?"

"Hunt everywhere for that key," Mannering said, urgently. "Press the bell for Simms again, he must be about somewhere." Even as he spoke he wondered if that were true. Lorna stabbed the bell-push, and then began to go through the things on the dressing-table, the mantelpiece and the dressing-chest, but he would not have put the key anywhere on its own, and he knew that it had been loose in his pocket.

Simms didn't come.

"If Simms took the key, he may have known about the room," Lorna said. "Perhaps it's open, and she's gone. Can I find out?"

"You'd lose yourself on the way," Mannering said. "I'll——"

"You're not going to get off that bed."

He knew that he could not do so without help, and was not sure that he could stand erect. He had never felt so useless, and never more aware of Lorna's strength of will. But there was fear in her, for the girl, and she said quite sharply:

"Tell me how to get to the room, I'll find my way somehow."

It was the only possible thing to do.

Mannering told her; and as he talked he realised how desperately anxious he was to find out what had happened; to know more about the crime with which Rodney had been charged; to know how Guy Vane was; to know what else had been discovered. But the urgent thing was to find out whether Hester was still in that room.

CHAPTER TWENTY-ONE

BLANK WALL

Lorna found the lift; the spiral staircase which led up from the landing by the lift and near the door and windows to the observation balcony. And she found the wall across the second spiral staircase. She looked at this as if by her will could make it fall as the walls of Jericho. The great stones which made the castle looked as if they would defy heavy artillery or rockets. She looked up awkwardly to the spot where Mannering had told her to look, and all she could see was a rough-faced stone. She began to press against this stone with her thumb, trying to cover every square inch of it, but the stone was twelve inches by nine, and it would take an age. She felt the soreness at the ball of her thumb before she was half-way through, and tried with her left hand.

She could not even see the keyhole.

She called out: "Hester Vane! Are you there?"

Her own voice seemed to come back to her from the thick wall.

She went over the top right-hand section again, but there was no result; nothing yielded to the pressure, and she could not see the keyhole.

She had to go back to John; he would have to tell Hennessy and Horton. She could not believe that there was no way to get into the tower rooms, that no one but Rodney had the keys.

As she hurried back towards the lift, she saw the doorway leading to the observation balcony, and stepped towards it. This was the nearest point anyone could get to the tower room, except up the spiral staircase. Wind struck at her as she stepped out. There was a parapet and, beyond, a sheer drop of a hundred feet or more. No one was in sight except, a long way off, cars on the road which led to Gilston.

Just to her left there was a tall, round tower, and it seemed vast and high above her. She could see a 'window'—little more than a narrow slit in the immensely strong walls. It was dark and narrow, too, and she could not see into the room beyond.

What must the girl be thinking about in there?

Hester was thinking despairingly: they're not coming back for me. They're not coming back.

Mannering could see from Lorna's expression that she had bad news. She closed the door sharply behind her and stood with her back to it. He had edged himself up so that he was sitting and leaning against the pillows, now; his back was aching, that was all.

"You'll have to tell Hennessy," Lorna said, without preamble. "I can't do a thing."

"Did you find the stone?"

"Yes."

"Did it have the keyhole on it?"

"John, it isn't any use, I searched every inch of that stone and found nothing."

Mannering said: "I see." Then he added very tensely: "At least, I'm beginning to see. Help me up."

"No, I——"

"I've got to get up there, even if I'm carried," Mannering said. "Help me up. I'll put some clothes on while you go for Horton's secretary. If she can't help, we'll send for Hennessy."

Lorna started to protest, but something in his manner made her move towards him. She steadied him as he put one leg out of bed, then the other; and she took his weight as he stood upright. His back seemed to break, and he gasped with the pain, but did not fall.

"Let me go."

"If you fall and hurt yourself——"

"Just let me go," he said, and she drew back, leaving him standing and swaying slightly, but he did not topple to one side.

"No worse than lumbago," he said. "Fetch Horton's secretary, will you?"

She turned away.

Very slowly, he began to dress; pulled on a pair of grey flannels, shirt, and a tweed coat, made no attempt to bend down to put on socks. but slid his feet into a pair of leather slippers; they were snug enough for him to walk in them. All that took him ten minutes, and should have taken two. Twice he pressed the bell for Simms, but no one came. It was as if with Horton's going nothing happened as it should. He was pushing his fingers through his hair when the door opened and Lorna came in.

"The secretary's outside, John, but she says that she's never even heard of the tower suite."

"Ask her to question all the staff, especially Simms."

"I've told the butler to do that," Lorna reported, and hesitated, and then said: "Largent is here."

Mannering looked at her unbelievingly.

"Horton sent for him to finish what you'd started," Lorna explained, "and—John, I wanted to give you more time to think about this, but Largent says that several of the pieces you said were fakes are real."

Mannering felt as if someone was kicking him. Then he began to move towards Lorna, his lips twisting wryly as he said:

"Largent doesn't make mistakes." He pushed open the door and saw a small, faded-looking woman, Miss Medbury, who had a scared, harassed manner as she looked at him.

"I do assure you that I've never heard of the tower suite, Mr. Mannering, but I've only been here for a few months. . . ."

"It's all right," Mannering interrupted. "Can you get me a walking stick?"

"Yes, but——"

"Bring it to the main gallery," Mannering said. "Is Mr. Largent there?"

"Yes, sir."

"Ask him to wait until I come," requested Mannering, and began to move towards the passage door. Lorna took his elbow as the secretary hurried off. "Darling," Mannering said, "go down to the car, and bring my tools. The special tools." He squeezed her arm, and almost unbalanced himself. "Sorry. I'll be all right. This is a job for the Baron without his mask."

"What do you mean?" Lorna asked sharply.

"That door revolves—I've seen it," Mannering said. "If you can't find the right spot to release the spring, then it's locked and the keyhole's concealed. I've got to find the lock and force it. I'm more likely to be able to than a local locksmith." He grinned. "Better have Hennessy here as soon as we can get him, it will be a change if a policeman actually sees me in action."

"I hope you know what you're doing," Lorna said.

"You get the tools, I'll telephone Hennessy."

Mannering watched as Lorna began to go ahead of him, glancing round as if she hated leaving him alone. He reached the side of the passage, stretched out his left hand, and steadied himself. Every step jarred his back, but the pain seemed less acute. He needed a local anaesthetic, something to ease that pain while he did whatever he had to do. Or something simple—like aspirins! He found himself grinning, tautly. He could not quicken his pace, and the thirty seconds' journey to the big gallery took him five minutes. He saw Largent there talking to Miss Medbury, and the little grey-haired woman was holding an ebony walking stick with a silver top.

Mannering saw Largent glance round; and saw the surprise in his eyes.

"Mannering, you oughtn't to be on your feet!"

"Got to be," Mannering grunted. "If I sit down again I'll never get up. Thanks." He took the stick. "Miss Medbury, get me Chief Inspector Hennessy, will you? Use that telephone."

"Yes, sir." The woman behaved like a little frightened sparrow as she picked up the telephone.

"I can't tell you how sorry I am about this," Largent said, and seemed genuinely embarrassed. "Horton asked me to come and help him as you were *hors de combat*, but if I'd realised that you were able to get about, I wouldn't have come."

He sounded as if he meant it. He was as striking to look at, in his sharp-featured, hook-nosed way, as Mannering.

"Forget it," Mannering said. He leaned heavily against the stick, while Miss Medbury waited for the police station to answer. "Would you mind getting some of the pieces I said were fakes and you say are genuine? That Louis statuette, for one, and the Genoese daggers."

"Mannering, I do assure you that I wasn't casting the slightest doubt on your—er—integrity. I suppose I could be as wrong as the next man."

"Mind if I look?" Mannering forced a smile as Miss Medbury bumped against him in her eagerness.

"Mr. Hennessy, sir."

"Thanks." Mannering took the receiver as Largent went to the nearer recesses. "Hallo, Hennessy." The other man sounded very deep-voiced as he answered: "Speaking."

"I was wrong and you were right," Mannering went on. "Miss Vane is in the Tower suite at the Hall. It's approached by a spiral staircase, which is blocked—as far as I know, only Rodney Horton could have locked it, but Horton himself might be able to. Will you ask the Yard to find out if Rodney Horton had a long, thin brass key in his possession?"

"Brass?"

"Yes—dull brass, with a complicated barrel," Mannering said. "No one would carry one about normally. If he had it, have it rushed here. If he hasn't, ask the Yard to question Lord Horton and find out if he can get into the Tower suite."

Hennessy exclaimed: "Good God! Do you mean to say you can't get in?"

"I'm going to have a damned good try, but this way would be simpler," Mannering said. "Hurry, will you?"

Hennessy said gruffly: "If anything happens to that girl, you'll only have yourself to blame."

"Could be," agreed Mannering. "Thanks." He put the receiver down, and saw Largent coming towards him with the statuette with the jewelled cloak. He did not handle it, just looked at it, and began to walk towards the far end of the gallery, and the lift. "This is one more occasion when you're right, anyhow," he said to Largent. "That's the genuine article."

"But *you* said——"

"I said that the thing I'd handled yesterday was a replica, and so it was."

"You mean——" Largent hesitated, gulped, and then went on with a rush: "You mean that someone exchanged it again?"

"Yes."

"But who would?" Largent's voice trailed off.

"That's what we have to find out," Mannering said. "Someone might be trying to cover up." He knew that he sounded ponderous; he felt ponderous, and his back was threatening to break in two. "Will you find out how soon Dr. Richards could come and give me an injection?"

"He's actually in the Hall, sir," Miss Medbury exclaimed. "Shall I go and speak to him?"

"Please."

She hurried off. Mannering moved towards the staircase leading to the lift, leaning heavily on the stick. He tried to tell himself that a few minutes would not greatly matter, but wasn't convincing. He could not be sure whether the girl was alive or dead; he could not be positive what had happened, but he felt sure that he knew at least part of the secret now.

He crawled up, and eventually reached the lift.

"I've never been up this far," Largent said.

"Here's your chance, there's room for two," said Mannering. "Mind if I go in first?" He stepped inside the small lift and backed against the side; then Largent stepped in after him. "It goes to the Observation Balcony," Mannering explained. He set his teeth as Largent pressed the button, and the lift began to move; it did not jolt badly, yet it was agony to his back. It was almost worse waiting for the jolt when it stopped. Largent stepped out into the passage, and saw the door of the second, smaller, spiral staircase was just in front of him.

That wasn't all.

He could smell burning.

He did not realise what it was at first, but felt the sharpness against his nostrils. Then he glanced towards the balcony, the doors of which were wide open, and he saw the smoke drifting by it.

Hester woke from a kind of dazed sleep, and like Mannering, was only vaguely aware of the smoke. It was as if she was dreaming of a fire. She turned over in the chair, and tried to keep her eyes tightly closed; it was better not to wake fully, better to stay like this as long as she could. But the smell of smoke persisted, and soon she opened her eyes.

Then she saw that the floor by the wall was burning, smoke was coming up through cracks in the wooden blocks, and here and there was a lick of flame.

CHAPTER TWENTY-TWO

THE BARON AGAINST TIME

Largent said in a scared voice: "It's coming from the tower, pouring out of the arrow slits. How could a fire——"

Mannering said swiftly:

"Rush downstairs and call the police. We need a fire-fighting unit, turntable, and everything necessary to make a hole in that tower wall. We want a pneumatic drill, too, get one here as soon as you can. Talk to Hennessy."

Largent was already at the door of the lift.

"Right!"

"Ask my wife to hurry!" Mannering called after him, and the lift door closed on Largent's answering word.

Mannering went towards the door which blocked his way.

The smoke seemed very pungent, but was no more than a thin mist here, partly because the breeze from the Observation Balcony drove it in. He felt in desperate haste, but could not hurry. He reached the wall. When he had last come here he had found it heavy; now he could hardly push it, and the hinges seemed rusted, the door seemed to scrape along the floor. He gritted his teeth as he put his weight against the studded oak, and at last it was open wide enough for him to squeeze through.

The smoke was thicker, and it seemed very warm.

He gripped the metal hand-rail, and began to pull himself up. The strain at his back was unbelievably painful, but he had to get up. He leaned against the wall as he pulled; the chief trouble came when he tried to raise a leg to get on to the next step.

The way the staircase curved, narrow close to one wall, wide at the other, making his task more difficult. Once he slipped, and groaned aloud with the pain; but he did not stop.

He began to cough.

It was very dark in here; the only light came from two of the arrow slits.

He could not see the wall for what seemed a long time. Normally he would have been there in a few seconds; now it seemed to be an age, and there was no sound but that of his own movements.

At last he saw the wall.

All the time, he was blaming himself for having agreed to leave the girl here; for bringing her. He had only himself to blame. If she died——

She mustn't die.

But he could not be sure whether the smoke was coming from the sanctuary which had been turned into a prison and might be blazing.

He reached the top step, where Lorna had stood, and saw the stone which Rodney had touched, to work the miracle of the revolving door; and it would be a miracle, now.

He looked tensely for the keyhole—or something which might conceal one. He needed a bright light, and there was none. He felt his pockets for his pencil-torch, but it wasn't in this coat. His eyes were watering from the smoke, and he kept coughing; each spasm racked his body, but he was hardly aware of pain.

He scrutinised the face of the wall blocking the staircase, and the well itself. The keyhole must be within hand's reach, so it would not be too high. The most likely place was between some of the great pieces of stone; these had been cemented together, and the cement would be easier to pierce than the granite itself. He could not see any button to press, any switch, or any hole. One might be filled in, with some soft material; putty, plasticine, even plastic wood. If only he had a light he could find out more quickly.

He heard a sound behind him, and Lorna called: "John!"

"I'm here, come up."

He heard her slip.

"Careful!"

She didn't answer, but suddenly a bright beam of light shot out, showing the writhing smoke; she had brought the torch from the Rolls-Bentley. She came in sight, carrying the torch in one hand and the box of tools in the other: specialist cracksman's or locksmith's tools.

"Open the case and put it on a step," Mannering said, and was caught with a spasm of coughing; that seemed to hurt Lorna as much as it hurt him. "Take out—the long awl. Then shine—the torch on the wall about level with—my waist."

Lorna began to do what he said before he finished; and soon the long awl, like a shoemaker's awl but with a longer handle, was in his hand.

"Now take the screwdriver and scrape the plaster between the stone blocks, we're looking for a soft spot," he instructed, and began to probe with the awl. The most likely place was just here, it would be handy for anyone leaving the Tower Room, or approaching it.

Who else knew the secret of the room, and of locking the mechanism, except Rodney?

And how was the girl?

She might be suffocated by now.

Hester was picking up furniture and placing it on rugs which she had put over the floor boards which were smouldering, to try to slow down the burning. The room was thick with smoke, and there was no air from the tiny windows. She kept coughing, holding her stomach with the flat of her hands to lessen the pain.

Tears were running down her cheeks and she could not help herself.

She fought for life, and all the time she thought: "They've put me here to die."

Mannering saw the blunted point of the awl, which had been pushed against the unyielding cement so often. He was a step lower down, now, and Lorna one below that. No one else had come, and he could not understand why. The man he wanted was Hennessy, with news that the fire-brigade were here, and that someone was on the way with a pneumatic drill.

Supposing one was brought?

Only one man could work on the wall, and the space was so confined and the smoke so thick that he would only be able to work spasmodically. The smoke was much worse, and he and Lorna were coughing against each other. His throat was parched. Oddly, he did not feel much pain at his back, it was almost as if the exercise had helped him.

Why hadn't the doctor come?

In fact, no one had had time to act, yet.

Then the point of the awl sank between the stones, and he felt a moment of intense relief.

"Lorna!"

"Yes?"

"I've found what I'm looking for." A cough spoiled his excitement. "Go and—get a wet cloth. Put it round my face."

Lorna was coughing as she went down the stairs. Mannering kept prodding at the little hole; it was filled with plasticine or something soft and malleable, and he was able to hook it out. He bent down for the screwdriver, and his back seemed to break. He pushed the screwdriver into the little hole, and began to hook out the putty. The whole thing had been done with fiendish cleverness, someone had meant to make sure that no one discovered this.

He could just make out the size and shape of the hole; rather like a match-box.

The screwdriver was up against hard stone, now.

He went down a step, so that he could see inside; and picked up the torch. The bright light showed the metal and the tiny keyhole. He needed not tools but nitro-glycerine for the task. He hadn't a chance with the tools, it would take far too long.

Nitro-glycerine: the burglar's *aide*.

He heard a man's voice, and looked round, saw Dr. Richards looming through the smoke.

Mannering said: "Go and telephone the police again, say that I must have nitro-glycerine to blow a safe or strong-room."

Richards gaped. "*What?*"

"For God's sake hurry!"

"S—sorry," Richards gasped, and held out his left hand. "Here's a loaded syringe, you'll——"

He slipped; and dropped the syringe. Mannering heard it break, actually saw the liquid spill out of it and stain the step. Richards stood absolutely still, as if paralysed by horror at his own clumsiness.

"Go and tell the police I must have nitro!" Mannering roared at him.

Richards muttered: "Yes, yes, I'll go. Yes."

He went hurrying; and Mannering was alone again.

He bent down cautiously and examined the steel and the keyhole. He had come up against this obstacle often before. They were usually in strong-rooms and in big safes, and buried not in stone but metal. This mechanism must have controlled the swing door.

How long would it be before the nitro-glycerine arrived?

That was the only hope for the imprisoned girl, for it would be hours before the lock could be forced, as long before a hole could be made in the outside wall.

Hennessy was in his car, racing towards the Hall,

knowing that the fire-fighting unit was already on its way, and likely to pass him at any moment. It had problems; of water supply and of a turntable and extending ladder to get up to the tower, but he could do nothing about that. He had to see what was happening for himself.

The big, round-faced sergeant was by his side, and the radio fitted to the dashboard was switched on. A call came, sharp and clear.

"This is Gilston Police Headquarters, calling Chief Inspector Hennessy, calling Chief Inspector Hennessy."

"Speaking for Chief Inspector Hennessy," the round-faced man said.

"Further message picked up from Mannering at the Hall. Mannering has asked for nitro-glycerine to force a strong-room door. Over."

Hennessy said desperately: "Tell them there's a supply in the laboratory, taken on the Nettley job last week. Tell them to get it to me in a hurry, but be careful with the damned stuff."

The sergeant gave the message. . . .

The clangour of the fire-engine bell sounded as the first of the units drew almost level with him. He pulled in, to let it pass. He was near Vane's bungalow, and saw the big sign over the entrance to the greenhouses and grounds: VANE'S MARKET GARDEN. As he flashed by in the wake of the fire-fighting unit, he saw Alicia Vane at the window; she would realise that there was something wrong at the Hall, and would soon be on the way to find out what it was.

Alicia went running into the garden, calling Michael. He came hurrying from one of the greenhouses.

"A fire-engine's just gone to the Hall and Ted's following," she said. "I'm afraid it might be something to do with Hester."

"Let's get going," Michael urged, and swung round towards the van. "Now that Guy's taken the turn for the better I can't believe that anything will happen to Hester."

Alicia didn't answer.

She prayed.

Mannering was coughing less, because the wet cloth round his face kept the smoke away. His eyes seemed to be on fire, tears of pain were streaming from them. He heard Lorna coughing, and others, too; plenty of people were in the passage, but none would venture for long in the narrow confines of the staircase well.

Why the hell didn't the police arrive?

He heard a man call, then cough, then call again. The smoke was thicker. He turned round awkwardly, and then saw Hennessy; and Hennessy was carrying a small packet in his right hand, and coming with very great caution.

"Nitro?" Mannering demanded.

"Yes," Hennessy said. "You used to handling it?"

"I can manage," Mannering said. "What kind of container is it in?"

"It's flat—used on a breaking-in job by specialists."

"Just what we want," Mannering said, and then Hennessy drew level with him and opened the case. Lying in tiny grooves were small flat containers, rather like a minature book of matches to look at, and one of them was small enough to put into the keyhole.

Hennessy said: "Be careful with it!"

"I don't want to blow myself up any quicker than you do," Mannering said. "No key?"

"Horton says Rodney had the only ones. You—you insert this stuff. I'll lay on the electric cable for the concussion," Hennessy said.

Mannering grunted.

Hennessy went down the steps much faster than he had come up. Mannering heard a mutter of voices. He could think only about the girl inside the room, and the risk involved in blowing the lock. It was all right for

Hennessy to talk, and better that Lorna should think that they had time to use electricity to detonate the treacherous liquid.

Mannering knew that there was no time.

He must get the smallest container into the key-hole, put two others into the match-box size hole beside it, and pack it as tightly as he could with clippings of plaster and the plasticine. Then he must get down the well of the staircase, take what cover he could, and explode the nitro by simple concussion; by throwing a heavy tool at the hole.

A direct hit would do all that was necessary.

In this confined space, it was impossible to tell what chance he had of escaping alive.

Hester was lying by a window, where she had gone for a kind of illusory air.

She had been unconscious for five minutes, unaware that the carpets, the rugs and the furniture were blazing.

The fireman in charge of the telescopic ladder took one look at the tower and said:

"We'll be fifty yards short of that, sir, haven't got a chance. Only thing we can do is to work from that balcony. We could erect a platform there and get out to the tower windows, but it will take hours."

"It will take hours," a man echoed.

It will take hours reached the ears of the crowd waiting down at the base of the tower; reached the ears of Alicia and Michael Vane as they left their van and hurried to join the crowd.

A police sergeant said to another:

"The Vane girl's up there, Mannering said so. I wouldn't give her a chance in a thousand."

Alicia bit her lips, to keep back a scream.

Michael said: "I could kill Mannering in cold blood."

CHAPTER TWENTY-THREE

CONCUSSION

THERE could only be minutes to spare.

Mannering pushed the nitro-glycerine gently into the keyhole, and then with agonising caution, packed it with a wedge which he carried in his tool kit. Once it was tight, he put a large container into the bigger hole, but it would be useless to try to pack that. He jammed a small spanner in, to make sure that as much of the force of the explosion as possible went inwards, on to the lock.

That was all he could do.

He took three heavy tools from the case, and then backed down a step. It was going to hurt abominably to hurl the tools at the nitro-glycerine, and there was the awful risk that he would miss.

He went down another step.

The curved wall would enable him to find some sort of shelter, the danger was that in trying to move quickly, his back might hurt so much he would stumble into the full force of the explosion.

He weighed one of the tools in his hand; a pair of stainless steel pliers. He wanted a brick, he ought to have told Hennessy to bring something heavy to throw.

Well, he hadn't.

The torch beam shone into the hole, and he knew exactly what he had to hit.

He edged himself into position, and drew back his arm; the pain at his back was bearable. He drew his arm further back. It was like taking a coconut shy, with his life and the girl's as the prizes.

Nine times out of ten he would hit a coconut.

Crazy thought: coconut!

For God's sake get on with it!

He hurled the pliers; dodged; then slipped. He fell. His back seemed to break in two. If he had missed, he would never be able to get back and try again.

Then he heard the roar, then felt the blast and a sudden, terrible weight on his right shoulder.

Lorna was struggling to free herself from two policemen who were holding her back. She had come, choking and gasping, from the smoke-filled staircase, and for five minutes had been nearly unconscious. All she wanted was to reach John. She pulled herself free, but Hennessy was standing at the entrance to the staircase, blocking her path.

"Take it easy, Mrs. Mannering," he urged. "We're going to blow the wall down. Mr. Mannering's fixed the explosive, we're waiting for an electrician with a detonator. He's on his way. There's no need for you——"

At that moment the explosion came.

It began with a strange hissing sound and developed into a deafening roar. Lorna was pulled off her feet by the suction in the doorway and the narrow staircase. She was flung against Hennessy. He cracked his head against the stone corner of the door, and grunted as he fell. Lorna toppled on to him, but did not lose consciousness. The floor and the walls seemed to tremble and shake, and the roaring went on. She was so deafened and so breathless and shocked that she could not think, but gradually thinking returned; and she realised that John had been in there. She tried to get up. People were bending over her, soothing her. She fought them off, until she was on her feet. Pieces of stone and masonry, tools, cement and clothes were strewn about the floor. Firemen were already forcing their way through, and the smoke was very much thicker.

"John!" Lorna screamed. "John!" She tore herself free from the restraining hands and rushed to the staircase. It was littered with rubble, and the dust and smoke seemed to choke her. She saw the light of torches playing on the dust particles, and also the red glow of the fire. Gasping, choking, she raced up the stairs until she came upon one of the firemen, on his knees beside a crumpled figure; the figure of John.

Lorna flung herself forward.

Mannering's face was cut and bleeding, and there was a gash over his right eye, but although his coat had been torn from his body, he seemed to be in one piece; not blown to bits as she had feared. She saw the fireman lift him, and exclaimed: "Be careful with his back!" But that hardly mattered, he could feel nothing now. Other firemen were coming into the cramped space. The lift was too small, so John was carried down three spiral staircases in all. St. John Ambulance Brigade men were already near the gallery. Richards was there with his equipment, and Lorna knew that everything that could be done would be done.

Then Lorna heard Hennessy speak from a stretcher on which he lay:

"How's the Vane girl? Is she all right?"

The words were hardly out of his mouth before a man and woman came hurrying from the staircase near the lift; something in their expressions told Lorna that these were the girl's mother and father.

"Is she all right?" Hennessy seemed to be talking in a daze, as if he did not really understand what he was saying. Richards was bending over him, and giving him an injection.

"Is my daughter safe?" Alicia Vane demanded. Then she saw the rubble-strewn doorway, and exclaimed in horror, and before anyone could stop her, thrust herself towards the heat and smoke-filled staircase. Men were stumbling on the stairs, and one called sharply:

"Get out of the way!"

Alicia moved aside, pressing flat against the wall. She saw the legs and feet of a girl, coming towards her; two men were carrying the girl, a third was supporting her head and shoulders.

"Oh, God," Alicia whispered, and it was a prayer. "Hester, Hester my darling." Desperately she turned and staggered down the steps, so that she need not waste a moment of the men's time. Michael saw her and came hurrying, and as she fell into his arms, she said: "They've got her out but I think she's dead, I think she's dead."

Michael Vane kept his arm tightly about his wife.

The firemen came, carrying Hester, and immediately Dr. Richards cleared a path towards a couch on the gallery. They laid the girl upon it, and drew back. Richards went close to her, and her mother and father approached on the other side.

Michael breathed: "She's alive, Ally. She's not dead."

"Yes, she's alive," Dr. Richards agreed, briskly. "Most of the injuries are superficial, I'd say, but she needs to get into the fresh air. She'll be all right soon, you needn't worry."

Alicia was sobbing.

"How's the Vane girl?" Hennessy was demanding.

"She's all right," someone called.

Hennessy stopped muttering.

The passage and the balcony and the stairs leading to the gallery below looked like a casualty station. Men and women were on the move all the time, and among them was Largent. Lorna had seen John taken to an ambulance, and knew that he was on his way to Gilston Hospital. She knew that there was nothing she could do to help him yet, unless she could find out what had happened at the Hall, and what Largent was doing. She was near Largent when the firemen, their hoses snaking up the spiral staircase, put the fire out, and then began to bring down the damaged furniture and ornaments. It was Largent who exclaimed aloud when he saw a statuette in one man's hand, and he swung round to Lorna:

"Do you see that?" He didn't wait for an answer, but reached the man's side and took the statuette; he spun round excitedly. "This is it, this is the fake—your husband said there was one here. I thought he was trying to cover up a mistake, but here it is!"

"This real, or is it a fake too?" asked a fireman who was carrying a dagger with a jewelled hilt as if it were precious.

Largent took only a moment to say:

"That's a replica—and it's another piece that your husband had identified as false, Mrs. Mannering. The real pieces must have been kept in the Tower suite after they'd been stolen. Who——"

He broke off.

Someone exclaimed, as if in horror, and there was a sudden lull in the buzz of talk. The only sounds came from the staircase, and the footsteps of a man who was approaching with long, measured tread. It was Lord Horton. His face looked like a death mask. His eyes were glittering, the only part of him which seemed to be alive. He kept walking forward, and men pressed back against the wall, out of his path.

Behind him, pathetic in her helplessness, was Miss Medbury.

Dr. Richards said: "Barry! What is it?"

Horton must have heard, but ignored him. He went towards the spiral staircases. He trod on rubble and on thick dust. Plaster was crushed beneath his feet. He had never seemed more massive—nor so unreal.

The doctor stood in front of him.

"Barry, what's the matter?"

Horton looked at him, and then with a single sweeping movement, pushed him to one side. He staggered against the wall. Lorna caught the tension which was in the others. For the first time since he had gone, she forgot John. There was Largent by her side, staring at Horton as if in fear.

Horton reached him.

Largent exclaimed: "What—what's the matter? My lord, what——"

There, in front of policemen, firemen, the servants, the doctor, little Miss Medbury, and Lorna, Lord Horton shot out his long, powerful arms and crooked his strong fingers round Largent's neck, gripping so tightly that on the instant Largent made a choking cry, then seemed to stop breathing.

Lorna knew that Horton meant to kill the dealer.

CHAPTER TWENTY-FOUR

COOL REASON

LORNA thought that the vicious power of Horton's attack would be sufficient to break Largent's neck. She saw the murderous glint in the big man's eyes; then two policemen and a fireman rushed forward, and a policeman struck Horton on the nape of the neck, making him back away and release his hold. The others gripped his arms. He struggled for a moment, but realised that it was useless, and stood quite still. Largent was coughing and reeling back against the wall.

The big burly sergeant who had been with Hennessy asked Horton quietly:

"What made you attack Mr. Largent like that, sir?" The calmness of his voice and the ease with which the 'sir' came out were alike remarkable.

Horton looked at him with those burning eyes.

"He blackmailed my son into stealing from me," he said. "And so he killed my son."

"I'd like you to come along to the headquarters and make a statement, my lord," the sergeant said with the same calmness. "Will you come too, Mr. Largent, please."

"It's a fantastic lie," Largent croaked. "A fantastic lie."

"But I don't think anyone who heard him believed that it's a lie," Lorna told Mannering just twenty-four hours later. She was sitting in a small ward at the Gilston Hospital, and Mannering was lying flat on his back. There were bruises and cuts on his forehead and a gash on his right arm, but the worst injury was still his back; he had been told that it would be two weeks before he could walk with any comfort; a month more before he was completely recovered; but there would be no lasting harm.

He looked pale, but was in no pain. He knew just what had happened: that both the girl and her brother would recover completely; that Rodney Horton had died from his injuries; that Largent was under arrest on a charge of complicity in the murder of Clive Morgan. He knew that Hennessy was in a nearby ward, much worse injured than he, with a cracked skull. That Horton had hardly said a word to anyone since his attack on Largent; and he also knew that the thin-faced man who had attacked him on the gallery was one of Largent's runners, who had stated that he had worked with Morgan to make Rodney steal his father's precious treasures.

"Now that we know the key to it, that Largent was behind it, everything is simple," Lorna said. She felt completely relaxed for the first time since she had come to Gilston, and there was no frown, no hint of sullenness. The key to the staircase wall was found on Largent's runner. He'd been with Rodney just before the accident. And some of Horton's missing treasures were found in Largent's flat.

"All very neat," Mannering murmured. "And Horton nearly choked the life out of Largent."

"I thought he would break his neck."

"I wouldn't have been surprised," said Mannering, almost lazily. "What did Largent have to say afterwards?"

"He and Horton were hustled away too quickly, so I don't really know." Lorna answered. "I suppose you had a pretty good idea that Largent was the man you were after."

"Delectable thought, but it didn't occur to me," said Mannering, and his smile was even more relaxed. "I always thought Largent was too big for his boots, an unbearable snob and a peacock for vanity, but strictly honest. I still think he is."

"What on earth are you talking about?"

"Honesty," Mannering replied mildly. "There's one thing that doesn't fit in. Largent wouldn't have wanted Hester Vane locked away in the suite where the stolen treasures were stored. I don't believe he knew she was there. Only two people knew that—Rodney Horton, who wasn't likely to talk, and I."

Lorna asked sharply: "What are you saying?"

"I'm saying that I think Barry Horton would sacrifice Largent's life and reputation to whitewash the memory of his son," declared Mannering. "One good thing about the affair has been the way in which parents have wanted to protect their young! But the only possible reason for anyone to attack Guy was that the attackers had been recognised. The only reason to want Hester blamed for the murder was to give someone else, who had no alibi, a funk-hole. Rodney Horton is the only person who fits in everywhere. He was in the woods on the night of the murder. He was being blackmailed by Morgan, and wanted Morgan silenced. He was in the woods when Guy Vane was attacked. He knew Hester was alone in the Tower Room. He knew that I had a key, and arranged the attack on me—to kill me—and doubtless arranged for the key to be stolen. He knew that Hester, who was deeply in love with him, but would eventually realise that he had killed Morgan; it had to be one or the other, and it wasn't her."

"John! If you knew——"

"I didn't know much in the beginning," Mannering said, "but it became obvious once the real issues were made clear. Hester was standing-in for Rodney, who was using her as a go-between for Morgan. And Rodney was quite prepared to leave her to die. I haven't any doubt that he believed that if she were to die in the Tower, it would be taken for granted that she was the murderer. And—can you see the greatest cunning, sweet?"

Lorna said: "Tell me."

"Rodney took a few of the precious things, fairly openly, and admitted it. But he also took much more, and hid that away. Clive Morgan didn't know how big the thefts were—the amount of hush money he settled for proves that. Rodney was a much bigger rogue than anyone dreamed and we knew that he handled stolen jewels apart from his father's. He knew all the great collectors, the men who would buy without a word, and hoard the *objets d'art*—he had only to pose as a frustrated, hard-done-by youth to get away with it. The police as well as Horton and everyone would be looking for a bigs shot behind Rodney—but none existed."

Lorna didn't speak.

"The ugly truth is that Rodney was robbing his father right and left, using the Tower suite as a kind of safe deposit, sneaking different treasures out one at a time, and selling them to these collectors. Morgan knew a little of that and began his blackmail. He threatened to tell Lord Horton, and Rodney had to kill him. Hester Vane had shielded him, but we know now how readily he sacrificed her, hoping to save his own skin.

"The runner for Largent who gave evidence against Largent will have taken a bribe from Barry Horton, simply to save his family's name. Largent was just an easy victim—who actually bought goods from Rodney in good faith. Horton took advantage of that situation."

Mannering stopped.

Lorna said: "But the evidence against Largent will be overwhelming, darling. He actually had some of the Horton treasures. If you really think this is true, how are you going to prove it?"

"I'm going to make Hester Vane tell the truth," Mannering said. "When she knows that Rodney deliberately left her in that room to die, actually had

Simms start the fire which was to finish her off quickly——"

"Simms?"

"Who else could it be? The valet who stole my key vanished, and still isn't found," murmured Mannering. "The valet who was there to spy on all my movements. The valet who had served Rodney for a long time. First the police want to find and then question Simms. If he doesn't break down, I'll tackle Hester." He closed his eyes. "I would much rather Simms were made to talk, I'd rather Hester didn't know what her lover tried to do."

"There isn't a word of truth in it," said Simms, who was caught in London that day. "I wasn't well on the day of the fire, and just stayed in my room."

Two weeks later Mannering stepped out of the Rolls-Bentley outside the Vane bungalow. They knew that he was coming, and he saw the curtain move, but was not sure whether the mother or the daughter stood there. Guy was still in hospital, but out of danger. Lorna, who had driven the car, came and joined him in the porch. He could move without real discomfort, but had to move carefully. Before he rang the bell, the door opened and Michael Vane stood there.

"Come in, Mrs. Mannering!" He looked eagerly at Mannering. "Mr. Mannering, this is the first chance we've had to tell you how deeply grateful we are to you. But for you, Hester wouldn't be alive, and——"

He broke off.

Alicia Vane came hurrying from the kitchen; so the woman at the window had been her daughter.

Alicia, trying not to let her emotion get the better of her, dabbed at her nose, and led the way into the front room. Hester Vane, completely recovered, was dressed in a slimly cut dress of pale green. She looked pale, but her eyes were very bright. She watched Mannering as if she were a little afraid of him, and her lips were unsteady when she greeted him.

"I'll never forget what I owe you," she said. "For as long as I live, I'll remember how right Guy was about you."

Mannering smiled as he gripped her hands.

"I helped to get you into the trouble, I had to get you out of it," he said. "Wouldn't you feel the same?"

She hesitated.

"Of course you would," Alicia Vane said.

Mannering was looking closely into Hester's eyes.

"It isn't always so easy," he said. "In some ways it would be better if Rodney were alive, it would be easier to tell the truth then, wouldn't it? Hester, Largent is awaiting trial. All the evidence is against him—including the evidence of your silence. Lord Horton means to preserve the memory of his son, and present him to the world as the victim of an unscrupulous criminal—of Largent."

"But that isn't the real Rodney, is it?"

"You believe he killed Clive Morgan, don't you? You believed he attacked Guy."

"It isn't true!" Hester cried, and there was desperation in her voice. "He didn't kill them, Simms did. Simms was the real devil, Rodney had to do what he ordered. Simms was blackmailing him as well as Clive. That's why I helped! It wasn't Rodney, he was tricked and cheated by everyone. Even now, you're trying to do the same to his memory."

The Vanes were standing very still.

Mannering said: "Tricked and cheated, Hester? If Largent is sentenced to life imprisonment for his part in the crimes, a part he didn't commit, he'll be tricked and cheated, and you'll have to live with your share of guilt. Simms could go anywhere and do anything, remember. He could contact Morgan, and if he was so deeply involved, why where you needed?"

Hester didn't answer.

"You were needed because Rodney had to have someone not concerned in crime to help him, someone innocent on whom to turn the police if anything went wrong. When Morgan began to press too hard and Rodney knew that he had to be killed, Rodney deliberately chose a time when you could be suspected, when you would be arrested. He was quite prepared to sacrifice you for his own ends. He hated his father and was prepared to sacrifice him, too. He used Simms, and anyone who might be helpful. You know that Rodney was simply an evil man, Hester. If you try to preserve the memory of a bad man, and if you condemn another to prison for life because of that memory, you will never be able to live with yourself.

"And remember, Rodney locked you in the Tower Room, deliberately. He left you to die.

"Don't try to be loyal to him any more, Hester."

He saw that she was crying.

"Yes," she said in a muffled voice, ten minutes later. "I was afraid that Rodney had killed Morgan. He was the only one near. But it was Simms who attacked Guy, I'm sure of that. It was Simms——"

Later, Guy described one of his attackers precisely, and it was certainly Simms. Challenged by that, Simms made a full confession; that he and Rodney had worked this out together for years. He and another man, Largent's runner, had attacked Guy because Guy had seen them among the trees, and crept after them, believing they were Morgan's murderers.

A week after that was established, the Mannerings were back in their Chelsea flat, and Hennessy came to see them. He was convalescent, but would be back on duty soon, and he looked bright and hale enough when in the room which overlooked the Thames.

"No, I won't have a drink," he said. "My head still plays me up a bit. A cup of tea wouldn't come amiss, Mrs. Mannering." Lorna rang for the maid, and there was silence in the lovely room, with its Louis Quinze *décor*, its gilt and its greys and blues. When the girl had gone, Hennessy said: "I've just come from Scotland Yard, I had a few things to clear up there. They're withdrawing the charge against Largent, offering no evidence. There's no doubt that Horton knew what his son was doing, and saw a chance to involve Largent. He just wanted to whitewash his little brute of a son, and nearly got away with it."

"How about Simms?" Lorna asked.

"He was in it up to the neck, as you suggested. Everything was pretty well as you reasoned, Mr. Mannering, I never thought I'd come to respect the lay mind so much!"

Mannering grinned.

"And I never thought I'd find a layman who could use nitro-glycerine as expertly as a safebreaker," Hennessy went on. "You wouldn't care to tell me how you learned to handle the stuff, would you?"

Mannering said promptly: "Of course. I once knew a man who. . . ."

Lorna was laughing at him over Hennessy's shoulder as he went on with his vivid imaginary story. It did not matter at all whether Hennessy believed it or not.